❧ *Racist* ☙

<u>Fiction Series</u>
The Alex Evercrest Series
The River Front
The Girl on The Grill
Missing
Maggot
Racist
Votive Candles
Windy City
Country Road
Pool of Blood
Sins of the Daughter
Body Parts
The Skull Collector
The Vanishing
The Shadow Fighter
Moonshine
Grief's Trajectory
The Magic Touch
Northern Lights
Alex Evercrest Heroine
Alex Evercrest Collection Two
New Direction
A Family Affair
Disruption
The St. Lebuinnus Church Murder

A Brian O'Neil Novel
Hawaiian Phoenix
Moon Curser
Death Broker

The Problem Solver Series
Solutions
Drug Lords
Border Crosser
The Problem Solver Collection

<u>The Taelo Series</u>
Taelo: The Early Years
Taelo: The Golden Feather
Taelo: Journey of Discovery
Taelo: Dangerous Passage
Taelo: Condor Clan Slingers
Taelo: Circumvention
Taelo: The Journey of Sages
Taelo: Collection
Taelo: Future Leaders Journey

<u>A Taelo Story:</u>
White Swan and Quiet Pheasant
The Child's Name
Floating Cloud
Quiet Rabbit
Busy Bee
Little Otter & Talking Wren
Broken Spear
Burley Bear & Meadow Flower
Taelo Story Collection

Science Fiction
The Savitar Series:
Journey's End
Savitar
Confluence
Savitar Series Collection

Bram Nielson Series
The Fold
The Message
Fold Wormhole
Negative Fold
Ripples in Time
Bram Nielson Collection

Single Science Fiction Books:
Current Past and Future
The Event
The Door
Viajante 7

Ron Mueller

Racist

By: *Ron Mueller*

Around the World Publishing LLC
Cincinnati, Ohio

This story is a work of fiction. Names, characters, places, and incidents either are products of the author's imagination or are used fictitiously. Any resemblance to actual events or locales or persons, living or dead, is entirely coincidental.

ISBN 13: 978-1-68223-335-1

Distributed by Ingram
Alex Evercrest Model By: Pi03@ShutterStock
Cover Picture by: Rimond@ShutterStock
Cover Design By: Ron Mueller

Dedicated to everyone who faces discrimination.

Table of Contents

Ron Mueller

1: Shooter

Paul had planned this attack for several months. His friends on the force had shared stories about the new black female detective. It pissed him off that she had earned the name "Cincinnati's Black Annie Oakley." The fact that she had also earned the respect of his longtime friend on the force made him even madder.

He learned that she had now shot and killed more "bad guys" then all of the police department.

She was thought of as a phenom!

He wanted to think of her as dead.

He had no idea why he had decided to take her out, he had put a good deal of thought on how to do it and how to not get caught.

He spent a good amount of time in learning her movements.

The fact that she rode her bike into work and back to her apartment each day led to his plan of shooting her as she rode into work.

From the group of acquaintances and friends, he recruited a driver and a shooter.

He then sat with them in the getaway car and watched their target ride by them for several weeks.

He would have loved to do the shooting, but he wanted to make sure that he would be able to deny any association with the shooting.

The shooter and the driver would use a sanitized old pickup truck that he had painted a bright solid blue for the shooting.

Sanitized meant all serial numbers on every part on the truck had been ground off. He had personally dismantled, ground off any serial numbers and rebuilt the truck. He figured no one would ever be able to link the truck or any part on the truck to any manufacturer and certainly not to him.

His buddies would abandon the truck a few blocks from the shooting and transfer into the car they were currently sitting in.

The shooters were passionate racists and voiced their gratitude for having been selected to take her out. The driver was pleased to have been selected. Neither cared that she had not done anything to them or their friends.

She was black and in a position of authority.

That was enough.

Paul set up a camera on the top of the truck cab to take in the shooting. This would give him a shooters view of the encounter, and he figured it would be highlighted by the bullet riddled body of his target.

He was looking forward to watching the shooting happen.

He planned to park nearby and personally watch the event. He would be on foot and appear to be a pedestrian. After the shooting, he would have breakfast at a nearby diner and then leave the downtown later in the morning.

It was a perfect setup.

He had invited his two accomplices to a late celebratory lunch after the shooting.

He figured that they would have a few beers and celebrate their accomplishment.

He parked his car in a parking area a few blocks from the shooting site. He walked slowly along and then stood at the intersection a block away from where the action would take place.

He was enjoying the early morning sunrise. He hoped he looked like an early morning riser on the way to breakfast. He could see the pickup, but Jeff and John were not visible.

He hoped they were as ready as he was.

In her apartment, the morning light played on her eyelids pulling Alex forcefully from her dream. She had been running through the woods trying to avoid the thugs chasing her and Matt through the woods.

Every time she thought she had succeeded a red laser bead would appear somewhere on her body and she zigged in a new direction.

This she knew was a nightmare. It was a nightmare because she had no control and could not manipulate its outcome.

Her abrupt awakening had her breathing hard, and she was sweaty. She walked into the adjoining bathroom and turned on the shower. She threw her damp night clothes into the hamper and stepped into the steamy shower and let the water flow through her hair as she stood and absorbed the heat.

She hated to wake up in this manner.

Her senses were on edge.

She recalled the most recent action that she had experienced and tried to get the premonition of trouble out of her mind.

She told herself to take it easy. She had just recently been reinstated and had not yet picked up a new assignment.

She had been doing routine work for the last several weeks. The Chief had intentionally been keeping her workload light.

She and Trey had gone through a tough experience in their last case and were happy to take it easy.

Trey had nearly been beaten to death and she had faced a battle with two helicopter gunships sent by a key Drug Lord.

They were both celebrating their survival.

She appreciated the lull in the work assignment but both she and Trey were ready for regular duty.

It seemed that regular duty for them was never regular but hyperactive.

She wondered what the next assignment would entail.

She turned off the shower and dried off, got dressed into her cycling clothes and walked into the kitchen.

As always she would ride her bike to work. She had several routes that she randomly chose to ride on the way to and from work. She took her bike down from the rack that she had hung it up on and quickly checked it out before pushing it to the elevator.

Once out on the sidewalk she decided on the route she would ride to work. Her cautious approach was based on the fact that she did not want to give any adversaries the advantage by being too routine in her actions.

She put her backpack on her back and her water bottle in its holder. Her black heavy duty helmet matched her bike in its sleek appearance. It was a special helmet recommended by her bicycle shop owner for its durability and its high impact protection.

This morning, she noted one early morning person standing on the corner as she rode toward the library. She was moving smoothly along when something hit her and knocked her of her bike.

She heard the sound of the shot immediately afterwards.

She hit the ground and let her elbow pad absorb the impact as she rolled over and behind the car parked in the street in from of the library entrance.

She immediately move up on the sidewalk and to the rear wheel of the vehicle.

The sound of a second shot put her into her defense mode.

She leaned tightly against the car.

The shooting now took on what seemed to be a continuous, machine gun like firing.

She managed to get her revolver out of her backpack.

She was hugging the side of the car, at its back wheel. She reached down and adjusted the spinning hub cap so that it closed the area around her thighs. She could feel where the bullets were bending the metal of the car out towards her.

She hoped the car would continue to provide her the protection she needed. She lost count of the number of dents that she could feel up and down her body. She wondered how many shots had been fired. The rear tire had taken several hits and the tire was flat.

The shooting seemed to go on forever. She wondered how many were doing the shooting. She moved her gun to her left hand. It would be the hand that would be the most versatile to shoot with at those doing the shooting as they drove by.

She waited until the truck went slowly by.

The shooting continued.

She glanced through the car and saw that the truck was about to turn the corner and the single shooter was off balance.

She stood up and took two shots at the shooter.

As he fell she put two more shots through the back window of the pickup.

She then ran out from behind the car toward the blue pickup.

The pickup swerved as it turned the corner, hit a parked car, and rolled over.

She took the time to reload her gun and then cautiously walked toward the pickup.

As she was walking toward the pickup police cars, sirens blasting and lights flashing seemed to come in from all sides.

She held up her badge and walked to where the shooter was down on the street. She kicked the rifle a few more feet away and then walked to the pickup to check on the driver.

She then put her gun on the ground and put her hands up in the air but held her shield up so that the approaching officers could see it.

She almost gave a chuckle when one of the officers shouted out "It's our Annie Oakley." She would have to tell Matt who had given her that moniker that it had come full circle and was now how she was recognized.

She followed one of the policemen to the emergency vehicle. It turned out that Matt was one of the EMT members. He asked if she was hit.

When he took off her helmet, he let out a whistle and pointed to the hole that went in just above the forehead and then at exit point that had blown off most of the back of the helmet.

She took the helmet in her hand and walked to where her bike was still in the street. The pickup had run over the front wheel. She pulled the bike up on the sidewalk. She set the helmet and backpack behind the bike.

The condition of her bike and helmet made her mad.

Then she returned to the street to take in all the bullet holes in the side of the car.

She put her hand on the car and thanked it for giving up its life to save her.

The Chief and Trey arrived together in the Chief's car. The Chief had a brief discussion with the senior policeman in charge and then walked to where she was sitting on the library wall along the hedge that was at the entrance.

When he asked if she was alright, Alex handed him her helmet and responded that it was her lucky day and she planned to buy a lottery ticket.

The Chief handed the helmet to Trey who looked at it and handed it back to her. He asked her to buy him a lottery ticket as well.

She smiled. She and Trey had been through so much together that she could sense his uneasiness at the three of them being in the open.

She stood up and led the way back into the street to look at the side of the car. It looked as if there was a bullet hole in every square inch of the side. She then walked back around to the sidewalk side of the car and counted the number of bumps that would have been bullets that would have hit her had they made it through.

She took in the fact that the rotating hub cap would never rotate again because several of the fins were bent outward. They had stopped several bullets. She would forever think about rotating hub caps as friends.

She looked at Trey and commented that she thought they should outfit their assigned vehicle with rotating hub caps and that she planned to buy a half dozen lottery tickets.

The Chief came back and told them that they were going to go back to the office. Her bike would be brought to the station, and she would be debriefed there.

She nodded and picked up her backpack. She then pointed to a hole that had gone into and ripped out a huge hole as it exited. She opened her backpack and groaned.

Her new laptop had a crease along its length.

She placed her helmet behind her bike and her backpack next to her helmet. They would all need to be processed before she could get any of them back.

Paul had watched in stunned silence as the shooting scene unfolded in slow motion. The first two shots hit their target, but he watched as she rolled, reached into her backpack, and crouched hugging the side of the car. Jeff was shooting in an almost continuous manner as the bump stock turned his AR-15 into a machine gun.

The pickup slowly approached the car, and the shooting was continuous.

Then he was amazed as the target stood up fired four shots as the pickup took the corner. She hit her mark on each shot. Then the pickup rolled on its side.

Four shots and it seemed that both Jeff and John were either dead or incapacitated. For his sake he hoped they were dead.

He could not believe that anyone could shoot like that. He had not known she was left handed.

He changed his plans and decided to get to the getaway car and drive it away.

He had under rated his opponent. She was more capable than he had given her credit.

In fact, Paul didn't know many critical things about the person that he singled out to kill.

To his own detriment he had erroneously selected the deadliest enemy possible.

He thought he would lay low for the near future but what he did not realize there was no place to go to and lay low.

2 Library

Johnnie was sipping on a cup of coffee, reading the morning paper. He had his police monitor on. He followed the dispatch calls but seldom had any reason to focus on the chatter that transpired between the dispatcher and the various units that were patrolling the city.

Thanks to Alex he was currently enjoying the best time in his life. He had survived Vietnam only to become an outcast on his return. The treatment he had received on his return had saddened and later made him somewhat bitter.

The younger population were derisive of his involvement, and the older population just followed their old habits of looking at his skin color and discriminating.

It was a lose-lose situation for him.

Alex had changed the downward trajectory of the path he had been traveling to an upward one.

He was now an official computer investigator for her and her department.

He also held a full time position as the apartment manager in the apartment building he and Alex both occupied.

The apartment owners liked his work, and he was now on the first floor in a newly renovated single room apartment.

She was in a sixth floor two bedroom corner unit. It was one of the best units in the building. Her fourth floor unit had been literally blown up by the angry mother of the hoodlum that Alex had shot and killed.

That was the hoodlum that had tried to kill him.

When Trey had been incapacitated on the last case, he had stepped in to be her partner.

It had given him a firsthand look at the type of honest, forthright person that she was.

It had also opened his eyes to her unwavering belief in being fair but taking the action that was required.

She left a trail of bodies of those that had chosen wrong.

Her swift actions had save both of their butts.

When the dispatchers voice changed and called out that shots had been fired, Johnnie put down his paper and leaned toward the radio as if it would improve his hearing.

The location and the time of day made Johnnie stand up.

He knew almost immediately that Alex was involved.

It was almost at the exact spot where he had first flagged her down on their first meeting. He did not wait for any more information but grabbed his cap and his identification and headed out the door.

He jogged toward the library.

He saw all the flashing lights and the EMT vehicle parked in the street by the library.

His heart was racing as fast as his legs were moving. He hoped any heart attack would wait.

He pulled out his badge as he approached the taped off perimeter. The officer on the walk was about to turn him down when Matt called out that he was with him.

He walked over toward Matt.

He saw the bike on the sidewalk with the front wheel smashed. Behind it was the damaged helmet. Next to it was a badly damaged backpack.

He looked at Matt before asking about Alex. Matt looked at him and said that Alex was fine and had been escorted by the Chief and Trey back to the station.

Johnnie sat down on the rear EMT vehicle bumper. He was out of breath but now able to relax and take in the rest of scene.

After a moment he asked for some gloves and then walked over to the car that was being examined. He looked on in amazement at the number of holes that covered the side.

He then walked over to where the blue truck still lay on its side. The body was still on the street where the coroner and his team were examining it and getting ready to bag it.

The coroner looked up and greeted him.

He commented that Alex was a deadly shooter that seldom missed. He speculated that she had wasted her second shot to the shooter. The first shot had done its job.

He pointed to the pickup and commented that he was pulling the second body out in a moment. He shared that he had overheard several of the police comment that it was a clean pickup with no identifying marks.

Johnnie walked over to an officer that was standing behind the pickup. He introduced himself as Alex's personal scene investigator.

He had no clue what his official title might be, but he smiled to himself when the officer seemed about to salute him.

He wanted to laugh at the immediate and helpful response he got. He would have to let Alex know of her strong influence with the police force.

The policeman said he could not believe anyone could survive being shot off her bicycle, take over a hundred incoming rounds and then take out the shooter and the driver with only four shots.

"Superwoman," is what he said everyone should call her.

Johnnie said that he agreed.

The he looked at Johnnie and waved him toward the truck.

Johnnie thought back to the time he had shared a meal at the shelter with an old convict that had claimed he had been a cleaner for one of the Mafia.

Johnnie had listened to the stories the old man had to share.

He now remembered that the most often missed spots were the wheel tie rods, the radiator, and the distributor rotor. They were not so much missed but thought of as parts that were not a permanent part of the car.

The parts, though not a permanent part of the car, were the breadcrumbs that could be followed to the people buying them or to junk cars that could be located.

Johnnie quickly eliminated all but the distributor rotor.

He stood back as the body was removed from the pickup.

Almost immediately afterwards the pickup was righted and positioned for transport to the holding area.

It would be thoroughly processed and most likely dismantled by a team trying to get evidence.

Johnnie borrowed a pad and pencil and wrote a note that he taped on the dashboard.

He let them know that he wanted the rotor bagged as evidence.

He walked over to where Matt and his team were putting away their gear.

He asked Matt if he had a message for Alex.

He listened as Matt told him that he wanted to have lunch with her.

Johnnie suggested that Matt bring several pizza's to the station. He was sure that the Chief would have all of them busy well past the lunch hour.

He then turned and walked toward the station. He noted that the bicycle, helmet, and backpack were gone. A second truck was loading the car with a hundred holes onto its bed.

He picked up his pace. He wanted to make sure that the Chief had some folks participate in the inspection of all the on the scene evidence.

The Chief had Alex and Trey in his office. Johnnie also saw Bill so he figured Travis would also be in the office.

He knocked on the door and then stepped in. The Chief nodded and waved him to a chair and asked him if he had any firsthand info.

Johnnie smiled and responded that his favorite detective always left an intriguing and challenging trail.

He went on to share that the pickup had been cleaned by a professional. He had checked all the usually missed identification marked locations and they were down to the distributor rotor and contact posts. He shared that the pickup and car were both on the way to the holding area. He suggested that someone on the team should be present when the inspections took place.

The Chief nodded and replied that he had assigned Bill and Travis to that duty, and he was now assigning him as well.

Johnnie nodded and said they should be getting out to the holding area or the shop where the truck would be dismantled.

He stopped to let everyone know that Matt was showing up at noon with pizza and drinks.

The Chief nodded and pointed at Bill and Travis and told them to pick his brains about where to find the identification for the pickup.

Johnnie stood to go. He looked at Alex and asked how she was feeling.

She smiled and replied that she was counting on one of his miracles. She had no clue who was out to get her, but she was feeling fine.

Johnnie smiled and replied that the guy out to get her would bring the pizzas for lunch and that she should get them all into a conference room to enjoy them.

3 Swiss Cheese

The Chief had kept the workload low on Alex and Trey. They both had gone through several tough cases and deserved a break. Luckily not much was happening. He enjoyed a quiet evening and expected a routine day.

Alarm bells went off when the first thing that caught his attention was Trey sitting and sipping coffee by himself.

This had never happened before.

He asked were his partner might be. Trey just shook his head and had a concerned look on his face.

He replied that she had not answered her phone.

Bruce walked into his office and put down his briefcase. He was about to open it when the dispatcher announced gunfire outside of the library.

He knew immediately it involved Alex.

He turned and ran out of his office and called out to Trey to follow him as he headed for his car.

The shots were still going off as he got to his car.

It sounded like a large-scale gun battle.

He was actually relieved to hear the continuing gunfire because he was now more certain that Alex was involved and that she must still be alive.

He put on his lights and siren and gunned the car out of the parking lot.

As they turned the corner, he caught a smile crossing Trey's face.

He looked where Trey was pointing.

He saw Alex was walking the scene in her riding outfit with her helmet and riding shoes still on.

He felt a surge of relief and a surge of pride in the one officer that had changed the environment of the detective unit and the police station as a whole.

There were multiple police cars in all directions and the yellow tape was being put up.

Trey got out of the car and walked quickly toward Alex.

He held back to let the two greet each other. He saw Trey give her a hug and step back and look around. It was clear that Trey was in awe of the scene.

He looked to where the EMT vehicle was parked and saw that Matt was standing and watching in an unconcerned way.

He knew then for certain that Alex was not hurt.

He was not sure of what had happened but the person he had been worried about seemed to be in charge.

He walked up and loudly asked who was in charge.

Everyone pointed to Alex.

He smiled and nodded.

He looked around and asked for the senior police officer to come to him.

He officially turned over control of the scene to him and told him he was taking Alex to the station.

He had not expected any objections and got none.

He then walked over to Alex and watched as she pointed to the hole in her helmet that entered just above the forehead and exited through what was left of the fin at the back of the helmet.

He realized that she must have been moving faster than the shooter had anticipated.

The shooter's miscalculation had cost him his life.

He suggested that the helmet be put behind the bike that was up on the sidewalk.

He watched as Alex nodded and walked to the back of the bike. She picked up her backpack and stopped as a pencil fell out of the bottom.

She knelt down and pulled out her new computer that had a shiny crease along the lid.

A second bullet had entered the backpack been deflected by the computer and blown out the bottom.

He thanked the Lord for a shooter that was not skilled enough to adjust to a fast moving bike rider.

He asked Alex again if she was alright and if she had been thoroughly checked out by the rescue squad.

She replied, her helmet, her riding gloves, her right elbow, and knee pads and now her backpack and her new computer, the items she counted on had all taken a hit.

She stood up and shook her head and said she was pissed and that she had killed the two people she would like to torture. She looked at him and replied that other than wondering why she had been targeted she was fine.

He was walking with her back towards his car her when the bullet riddled car caught his eye and stopped him in his tracks. It would have been an understatement to say it looked like Swiss cheese. It had so many holes that it made him wonder how Alex had been able to come out without a scratch.

Trey was crouching down and looking under the car. He stood up and asked Alex if she was sure she had not been shot.

The Chief looked over at the bullet riddle car and asked Alex if she was sure she was OK.

The Chief walked over to Matt and told him he was taking Alex to the station and that he was welcome to be there if he wanted.

He nodded when Matt said he would likely come at lunch time.

He walked over to where both Alex and Trey were standing and looking at the blue pickup and watching as the coroner's team put the second body into their vehicle.

The coroner came over and smiled as he told Alex that she should be more frugal and that she had wasted two bullets.

He added that he was glad that the provider of bodies that kept him employed was untouched.

He made a comment about getting back to the office for a first cup of coffee and a review of the morning events.

The chief looked around and commented that he was personally very interested in hearing Alex's side of the story, and it was time to get to the office so he could listen to the account from her point of view.

The three of them walked back to his car and Trey opened the passengers door so that Alex could get in.

He drove slowly back to the station.

It seemed that everyone had learned about Alex's encounter with the shooters and they were all at the entrance area and cheered when she got out of the car.

He led the way through the crowd and turned to go to his office.

He nodded when she excused herself and said she was going to change into her everyday work clothes.

He led the way to the coffee center and poured out two cups of coffee.

He asked Trey how Alex liked her coffee. He watched as Trey poured in the cream to make it look a pleasant light brown. They both walked to his office.

Alex walked in holding her riding outfit in a large evidence bag that held everything including her riding shoes. She said that there was no hurry with her things. She figured she was going to have to replace everything.

She figured the bike would need a new wheel; front wheel and a frame alignment and she would get that done as soon as she got the bike back.

He nodded when she volunteered that she did not have a clue why she was attacked.

He stood up and signaled to Bill and Travis to come into his office.

Bill immediately gave Alex a hug and told her he and Travis were relieved when they heard she was alright and that they were ecstatic about her nailing the shooter and driver.

Travis uncharacteristically gave Alex a hug as well and followed with "it would have been hard on me to lose the one person that makes my day."

Bruce was just about to start when Johnnie knocked on the door and entered.

Bruce looked around at the people in his office and knew that the perpetrators that had thought about and set up the shooting were about to face an onslaught that they had not anticipated.

The result would be worse than hornets seeking the person who had thrown a rock into their nest. This swarm of hornets had a deadly queen bee with a terrible sting.

The Chief knew that once on the trail, Alex would be as relentless as a good hunting dog on the trail of a raccoon. Even if the raccoon jumped tree to tree that hunting dog would capture its prey.

4 Rotor

Trey had enjoyed an early morning breakfast with Lindsey and was expecting to take ribbing from Alex for being a little later than usual. He got his usual cup of coffee and walked into the bull pen.

Alarm bells went off.

Alex was not at her desk.

He was now on full alert.

He just sat down when the Chief walked in toward his office. He watched as the Chief looked around and then asked about Alex.

He shrugged his shoulders and shook his head.

It seemed that as soon as the Chief went into his office the call about shots fired near the library came over the speakers.

He was up and the Chief signaled for him to follow.

He was relieved by the fact that there was not an "officer down" as part of the shots fired announcement.

He was sure that it involved Alex.

When the car arrived at the scene, he was relieved to see Alex commanding the scene while still in her bike riding outfit.

He saw Matt standing by the EMT vehicle and knew that Alex had experienced another miracle.

The coroners vehicle was backing in toward where one body was being examined by the coroner.

He looked at the car that had its sides blasted full of holes. He looked under it and realized that Alex had crouched behind the rear wheel. The tire was flat, but she had somehow not been hit.

He walked up to her and gave her a hug and whispered that he believed in miracles.

This was reinforced when Alex showed him where a bullet had entered her riding helmet and blown off the rear helmet extension.

He was examining it when he heard the Chief taking over the scene and putting the control into the senior officer's hands.

When Alex walked over to her backpack and discovered that a second shot had creased the cover of her computer, he was sure about miracles.

He walked over to where Matt was standing by the EMT vehicle and asked if he was alright.

Matt smiled and replied that being with Alex was being near the center of the storm. It was unusually quiet at the center, but you were surrounded by lightening, and high winds.

He commented that the last time he had brought his EMT team to where Alex had been, he had to transport her to the emergency room. At that scene she had left two bodies for the coroner. He said that he was satisfied to just watch her in motion.

Trey nodded and agreed.

He walked back to where the Chief was telling Alex that they were going to return to the station.

He put his hand on Alex's shoulder and told her it was his turn to put her in the front seat.

She smiled at him and made the point that she had to carry him when she put him in the front seat.

He agreed and thanked her for that time but this time he had coffee and half of a bear claw waiting at the other end of the ride.

He reminded her that she had abandoned him to a hospital bed.

The ride back to the station was quick and it was quiet.

He listened as Alex excused herself to go to the locker room to change.

He saw Sandra, a policewoman that had guarded Alex during the last case and asked her to go with Alex.

Sandra nodded and followed after Alex.

He and the Chief stopped by the coffee center just as Bob and Travis came in. The Chief told the two of them that he would be calling them in to be part of the investigation of the shooting and that he wanted them to be present when the two vehicles were examined.

Trey topped off the coffee with cream and looked into the box of donuts that Bill had carried in. He took the bear claw and put it on a napkin.

Bill asked if he thought she would eat it.

Trey looked at him and smiled and replied that she would only get a half, he was going to eat the other half to put him in a sugar high so he could calm down.

Bill laughed and replied that he ate donuts to give him enough energy to put up with his partner. He commented that he was not sure that half a bear claw would give him enough energy to keep up with Alex.

Trevor got into the exchange by commenting that being near Alex was enough to boost anyone's energy level.

Trey stood up when Alex came into the office and took the evidence bag that she had put her riding outfit into.

He handed her a cup of coffee and pointed to the bear claw and told she could have half.

She smiled and replied that she didn't need a sugar high, but she reached for the bear claw and ripped it in half.

Trey was relieved by the composure that Alex displayed and as always the stunning figure she made in her black pants suit.

His phone rang and he was going to silence it when he saw that it was Lindsey.

He excused himself and stepped out of the office. He let Lindsey know that Alex was fine and that he would invite her over so that Nolan would be reassured that she was OK.

He stepped back into the Chief's office and let Alex know that it had been Lindsey.

He looked at the Chief to see if he was OK with the interruption.

The Chief smiled and said that he had just taken a call from his wife probably asking the same question and that the real bosses were making sure Alex was being treated with kid gloves.

Trey then listened as the Chief handed out their assignments. He watched as Bill, Travis and Johnnie left.

Johnnie, Bill, and Travis wandered around the shop where the truck was being dismantled. The bullet riddled car was in the adjacent shop.

All three of them went over to look at it. It was a souped up Caddy with spinner hub caps. The crew working on it were still in the stages of just looking and counting bullet holes. They were on the second round and were painting each hole with a white temporary paint as they counted them. They said that on the first count they had lost count at one hundred forty seven rounds.

They figured it was a miracle that Alex had survived.

They had also counted thirty two rounds that had dents protruding out where Alex had been hiding. They speculated that had this been a newer car the bullets would most probably have gone through.

One of the techs pointed to the spinner hub cap that had kept the bullets from hitting Alex's legs. It was lucky that the spinner was in the closed position.

Johnnie commented that luck had nothing to do with it.

He was sure that Alex had positioned the spinner to the closed position.

It was clear to him that the spinner would never spin again.

It had stopped several bullets.

Trevor commented that he might rethink his constant teasing of Alex.

He was sure he did not want to get her mad.

Johnnie chuckled and told Trevor that he did not have to worry about teasing Alex, but he warned him about ever trying to shoot her.

The three walked back to where the blue pickup was almost fully apart. The engine had been placed on a stand and was being taken apart.

Johnnie asked the mechanic to take the distributor apart and was pleasantly surprised to see the serial numbers on the rotor. He took out an evidence bag and had the technician put the rotor into the bag.

He had what he wanted.

He excused himself and told Bill and Trevor that he was going to find out where the rotor had been sold and hopefully to whom.

He told them that he would see them over pizza at lunch time.

It took him at least an hour but the serial numbers led him to a parts store in Oxford.

He looked up at the clock and realized that it was close to the noon hour. He was going to the huddle room, to share his good news and have a couple pieces of pizza.

He arrived at the conference room as Alex led Matt into the room. The smell of the pizza's made his mouth drool.

He figured he was going to enjoy lunch and knew that his findings were important.

He listened as Matt shared the fact that he might have seen one of the perpetrators of the shooting.

The video that had been retrieved from the camera on the blue truck clearly showed a person standing on the corner watching the shooting and then quickly walking away.

Johnnie listened as the Chief called Matt's boss and had Matt relieved of his EMT duties for the next few days because he had become a potential witness.

Johnnie then shared what he had found. He was pleased when Alex walked over to him and gave him a hug and commented that he always came through with small miracles.

He commented that Matt could help him track down the buyer of the rotor that he had traced to a parts store in Oxford.

The Chief spoke up and said that neither of them would be doing any follow up investigation.

Johnnie would learn later that the Chief and Bill ended up checking out the parts store and tying the person purchasing the rotor to the one that had painted the pickup.

5 *Man on the Corner*

*T*he call came in of an ongoing gunfire. The library address and the time of day immediately sent alarm bells off in his head. Matt led his team to their rescue vehicle. He was sitting in the passenger's seat as they approached the scene of the shooting. He glanced casually at the person standing at the corner. This person was looking toward the library. Matt registered that it was early for someone to be out but then he turned his attention back towards the library.

His stress level was peaking.

He felt immediate relief when he took in the person standing at the intersection.

It was a figure that he would know anywhere.

He went to sleep dreaming about her and usually spent the day worrying about her when she was on a case.

When the truck stopped he jumped out. He hollered out to his team to set up, but he ran toward Alex. He looked her over to make sure she was not hurt and then gave her a hug.

He took note of the figure sprawled on the ground and surrounded by a pool of blood. He asked about any others and was relieved to hear Alex simply say, "dead."

He took her hand and led her to where his team was set up.

There were now police cars at every intersection and the yellow tape was being pulled into place.

One of the senior policemen came over to ask what had happened and who was in charge.

He watched as Alex showed him her badge and said that she was.

She was still in her biking outfit and the click-clack of her shoes as she walked away with the officer seemed to him to be extremely loud. He knew that he was still on the adrenaline high that the rescue call had given him.

The last time he had come on a scene that included Alex was when she had been shot by an angry father seeking revenge. She had used the mother as her shield when the angry father blasted away with a shotgun. The mother died from the shotgun blast. The father from a bullet between his eyes. When he and his team arrived, they found Alex passed out with the dead mother laying on top of her. They had rushed Alex to the emergency room.

The trauma doctor put her into a forced coma to relieve the stress of her wounds.

He barely remembered calling her mother, but he had stayed with her for the rest of the day.

He was holding her hand when she opened her eyes.

This time he gladly sat on the back bumper of the EMT vehicle and watched as she walked the police through what had happened.

He saw Trey get out of the Chief's car and walk out towards Alex. The smile he saw on Trey's his face was exactly how he felt himself at the moment.

He started to think through what had just happened. He looked back over to where the lone individual had been standing.

He was gone.

A flag went off in his head. He looked around to see if the individual was standing anywhere nearby.

Then the Chief walked over and invited him to lunch.

Then Trey came over and asked if Alex had been checked over.

The thought about the spectator who had walked away from the area evaporated.

It seemed that the team was not needed, and he got them to pack things up.

Johnnie came running up and was about to be turned away by the police officer, so he hollered out to that Johnnie was with him.

After a brief conversation, Johnnie suggested that he bring some pizza to the station at lunch.

He and the EMI team returned to the station.

He called and ordered three pizza's. The pineapple fruit mix that was Alex's favorite, he added an extra cheese pepperoni, and a cheese and sausage.

He ended the call and the vision of the guy on the corner flashed in his mind.

He thought through and tried hard to see the person's face. He felt that he would recognize the person if he saw him again, but he could not see him clearly in his mind.

He decided to write down exactly what he remembered. He would share this with Alex, Trey, and the Chief when he delivered the Pizza.

Later when he entered the police station, he stopped and watched Alex walk toward him.

It was a sight that always took his breath. She gave him a brief hug and said that everyone was in the big meeting room.

She took the bag with the cups, napkins and plates and led the way

Once the pizzas were opened, he reached into his pocket and pulled out what he had written and handed it to Alex.

Alex read it, looked at him and handed the paper to Trey.

Trey read it and simply said, "we have a witness," and handed the paper to the Chief.

The Chief read it and asked him if he were still on duty.

He replied that he was on his lunch time but needed to get back to the team.

He listened as the Chief talked to his boss and told him that Matt would be busy for the next several days. He had important visual information about a possible witness to the shooting.

Johnnie chuckled when he read what was on the paper.

He commented that he had invited Matt to lunch because he knew that he would be part of the team that was going to nail the guy.

Alex leaned over and kissed Johnnie on the forehead and simply said, "my magician can also foresee the future."

Matt heard Johnnie say, "let's play that tape again."

Bill stood up and went to the television and turned it on. Bill looked at Johnnie and told him it was not a tape but a digital recording.

Johnnie smiled and asked that Bill cut an old guy some slack.

The scene blossomed on the screen, and you could hear the shooting. Matt was amazed at what seemed like Alex's synchronized movement that had her rolling behind the front of the car while at the same time pulling out her gun. She then disappeared, but the firing and the roaring sound enveloped the room. The AR-15 fifteen sounded more like a machine gun than a single fire weapon.

Matt pointed to the tiny figure that could be seen on the corner where he had seen him when he arrived. Then the scene went on its side and the wheels of a car was all that was on the screen.

Trey made the point that the guy on the corner might be the master mind and was standing by to witness the shooting.

Matt made the point that he would know the face if he saw it in a line up.

Johnnie held up a distributor rotor in an evidence bag and suggested that a starting point was to locate the parts store that had sold the rotor that was in the distributor of the blue truck. He said that the buyer might well be the person on the corner or someone associated with him.

He speculated that the camera that had caught the person looking at the shooting scene and the "tape" in the camera at the and the camera at the parts store might show the same person.

Alex gave him a hug and thanked him for doing his magic.

Johnnie volunteered to find that store and get the security tape.

The Chief interjected that he was not doing any of the fieldwork.

Johnnie sat down next to Matt and told him that the two of them could make a huge difference in the case if they just would not be held back by the boss.

The Chief simply said there was no way he was going to risk Alex's miracle man.

He said that he and the rest of the team would take the lead and get the next piece of evidence.

<u>6 The Face of Hate</u>

*P*aul watched from one block down as the shooting began. He was amazed as he saw that the first two shots had taken the target down but that she had rolled past the front of the car and had positioned herself against the rear tire well. He saw that she had somehow gotten her gun out of her bag. He wondered about Jeff's ability with his AR-15.

He figured she would be taken out by the constant barrage of gunfire. The car she was hugging was shaking from all the bullets hitting it. He figured she must already have been hit several times, but she was not going down.

He felt that he was watching a time lapse series of photos as the pickup drove by the car and continuously put a stream of bullets into it.

He almost fell over when she stood up, positioned her left arm on the car roof, and shot Jeff. She then shot at and most likely hit John because the pickup swerved, hit the rear bumper of a car and rolled over.

The silence that followed and the fact that his target walked toward the pickup put him into a panic.

He knew that he had to get to the getaway car and get out of the area. The fact that he also had his car parked complicated the matter.

He chose to get to the getaway car. He did not want it getting into the hands of the police.

The four block walk to where the car was parked seemed to be more like a mile. He kept his hood over his head and resisted running. He hoped that he was not too exposed.

Once at the getaway car he decided to drive to where his car was parked and make sure that he was paid up for the day. He would come back later to get his car.

As he drove home he thought over on how he had come to take the action that he had.

He laughed at himself when he thought about standing in front of a judge and saying that his parents had made him do it but in fact they were the ones that had injected his mind with the hate he felt for persons that were Black.

He was pissed about how things had turned out and was wondering how he would stay out of jail. Jeff and John, even if they were dead would most likely have the police looking at him in some manner.

He arrived back at his shop and decided that he would need to get Fred to drive him back to downtown Cincy to get his car. But first he wanted to think through what he planned to do.

He decided to put the getaway car in the storage garage that he rented. It was where he had prepared the pickup. He would repaint the car and sell it as soon as possible.

He had a job that afternoon.

He figured it would be a good idea to see if Fred was available.

This would give him a way to have Fred take him to his car and it all seem like part of the work.

He did not want Fred to know anything about what was going on.

After the job he got to his car as planned and drove it back home. It was one of the few time that he drove the speed limit. He did not want to get a ticket and get noticed by the police.

The call from his father surprised him.

His father was praising Jeff and John for having tried to kill the black female detective. He made the comment that at least they were trying to take action.

He asked why he hadn't been with them.

Paul felt like choking his dad.

He realized that his dad had never taken action. He boasted about having left the clan because they talked too much but took no action, but his father had not taken action either.

He had taken action.

He thought he would be celebrating with his buddies. Instead, he would now be trying not to get caught.

He decided to go to his favorite diner and eat a meatloaf, mashed potato, and gravy dinner with several beer chasers. He had to think through what he should do next.

The next morning, he returned to the storage locker. He looked over the getaway car and decided to paint a blue strip from front wheel well to back wheel well. This would get rid of the blue paint he had left over. The painting took less than an hour.

He made a for sale sign and put the car by the street in front of the rental facility and returned to clean his locker area.

He was just pulling down the door when his phone rang and when he answered he found out that a woman was interested in the car.

It felt great to get an immediate hit.

He let her know that he was on the way out.

On his way past the dumpster, he threw his two black trash bags with all the materials he had just bagged during his cleanup and walked out to the car.

The buyer was a woman about his age. She made him an offer that was about ten percent lower than his asking price.

He commented that her offer was a little low and that he had put on a really good price.

He looked at her as she thought about it. She shook her head and raised her offer by a hundred bucks.

He would have let her have it for her original offer, but this was much more satisfying.

He held out the title.

She took out her checkbook and wrote a check. He would have preferred cash but figured that would have delayed getting rid of the car.

The drive home took him by the liquor store where he usually bought his beer. He walked in and was happy to see that the new clerk was behind the counter.

He picked up the case and walked to the checkout.

He decided he should make his move. He invited her out for a beer and a brat. She smiled and said that she would enjoy that and gave him the time she got off of work.

It seemed to him that things were ironing themselves out.

He had sold the getaway car and made a little money on it.

He had now gotten a date.

He drove home and carried his case of beer into the kitchen and loaded the door with six of them. He took out his last cold one and decided he would nuke a dog and enjoy a cold beer.

Paul sat and sipped his beer. He was still in shock about his friend's failure to shoot and kill the black detective.

He had never envisioned her to be such a steady, brave, and deadly person.

He had figured that a couple of shots would have killed her, and his two friends would have gone around the corner and disappeared.

Instead, what he had watched was a true warrior in action.

Her four shots had killed both of his friends.

He was sure she had evaded more than one hundred rounds from the AR-15 and had responded so efficiently that it had taken his breath away.

He had come back and cleaned out his rental unit in hopes that he could erase all connection between himself and the blue pickup.

He was now concerned with the fact that he had put all the trash into the dumpster at the end of the rental area parking lot. He should have known better but he was distracted by the call about his car.

He planned to go back on Monday and remove his two black bags.

He had sold the getaway car and felt good about that. It had been a cash transaction. Well, a check anyway. It would have been better if he had insisted on cash, but he figured it didn't matter since it would be impossible for the car to ever be found.

He took another sip of his beer and looked out at the lawn. It needed cutting but his house was in the country, and the nearest neighbor was at least a half mile away.

It could wait.

Damn, how could she have been so cool?

He had left as she walked to the corner and made sure that the shooter and driver were both dead. She was in a black bike riders outfit and looked very sexy. It was a look that he would now put in the deadly look category.

The EMT unit awakened him from his stupor. He had made his hasty retreat from the scene. It had been hard for him to think about what he should do next, but he knew that by getting the getaway car out of down town Cincinnati, he had taken the right action.

He figured he could relax. He might end up being questioned about Jeff and John, but he could truthfully say that they were just guys that he periodically hired to help him.

He figured when the cops checked on his background they would find that he was a private contractor with a clean record. He was sure that there was nothing else on record then maybe a speeding ticket.

He figured a call to his buddy on the Cincinnati police force might give him some inside information that would better prepare him for whatever might follow.

He decided to cut the grass.

The ride on the mower and a second beer cleared his head.

The yard looked great.

He had crisscrossed the mowing creating a great pattern.

He had several jobs lined up and he figured he would hire Fred to help him.

e really did not need Fred's help but figured it would be good to have a second person's support if he got questioned.

He would make sure that Fred had only good things to say about him.

He was pretty sure that Fred did not know either Jeff or John.

He figured he was ready for what might come his way. He would feel better once he got the two black bags that had his paint cleanup trash out of the dumpster and got rid of it in some other location.

He nuked another dog and was thinking about the coming Friday and his date with, Margery, the clerk at the liquor store when the ring of the phone startled him.

He picked it up and was surprised to be talking to someone in Mississippi. The person identified himself as a supporter of what he and his friends had been trying to do and that the black bitch had come to Mississippi and killed one of the members of their group.

The group had agreed to having a couple of their members come to Cincinnati and help him finish the job.

Paul laughed and asked if this was a police sting operation and how did he know that the call was on the level.

The caller on the other end laughed and told him that his father had called an old friend in Mississippi and told them about Jeff and John getting killed by the detective in question.

The person on the other end shared the plan to be in Cincinnati on Sunday to finish the job that he had started.

After agreeing to meet them in Cincinnati and getting linked to a website that featured the Mississippi group, "Patriots for A better Future," Paul agreed to meet the two members coming up to help him.

After he hung up alarm bells went off in is head. They had easily found him because his dad had called them. Who else had his Dad talked to and had Jeff and John talked to anyone?

He decided that he had to get ready to leave the area. He went to three ATM's and drew all of the money he had in his personal checking accounts and his two business checking accounts.

When he got back home, he went to the website that the Mississippi contact had provided and found the location of the compound. He figured that would be as good of a place to retreat to as he could think of.

He packed his bags and put them in the back of his pickup. He would go to Cincinnati prepared to follow his two new volunteers back to Mississippi.

Little did he know what awaited him and his two new hit men was something far different than what he envisioned and much more deadly.

7 Blue Stripe Linkage

The morning had taken its toll. Alex was exhausted. She had been the target of a planned assassination or killing. She had no clue how any previous case might be involved. Someone had it in for her and it somehow seemed random.

Matt's observation and recall had put some reality into the case but there was no way to get the case off the ground.

The Chief had sent her home after lunch and had assigned round the clock protection to her. She had thought about arguing but decided for herself that she might just need it. This was worse than when her fourth floor apartment had been destroyed by a rocket launched grenade. That situation was quickly linked to the angry mother of the thug that she had killed.

She looked through the peep hole to see who had knocked at her door. She saw Sandra and knew that she would be the day to evening guard.

She opened the door and jokingly said that no she could not have one of her chairs to sit on.

This was a joke between them about a previous case where Sandra had been assigned to guard her. She had given Sandra a chair to sit on, but the chair had been destroyed when the persons sent to kill her had fired a machine gun through the door from inside of the apartment and destroyed the chair.

Sandra smiled and held up a folding chair and said she had brought her own cheap chair but wanted to make sure that the shooters were not in the apartment.

Alex gave her a hug and told her that coffee was ready but anything else would have to wait until later and that she was going to take a hot shower to relieve her stress.

The hot shower was just what she needed. She was not bathing. She was unwinding. She planned to follow up with a long run in the gym.

She was just getting dressed when her phone rang. The church bell chimes let her know it was her mother. She had given her dad the sound of a large gong. Just the chimes brought a smile to her face.

Her mother said that the media had protected her identity but how many black female detectives did Cincinnati employ. Her mother asked if the EMT person involved was Matt.

Alex laughed as she asked if her mother wanted to join the investigative team.

Her mother replied that she only joined teams where she could be the center of attention and the center for this case was already occupied.

Alex then got serious and said that they had no clue why the attack had occurred. She pointed out that the Chief had put her under twenty four hour protective surveillance and that for once she had thanked him.

She turned down the offer to come home for the weekend. She shared that she was going to a grill out at Trey's house on Sunday.

Her mother was acquainted with all of her friends and extended her invitation to all of them. After some idle chatting they said their traditional, "Love You" and hung up.

The lunch pizza was still holding, so Alex decided to go run on the tread mill. She would have preferred running along the Cincinnati River front but knew that it was out of the question.

She prepared a tray of cookies that she would put into the oven when she came back from the gym.

She remembered one fishing day out on the lake with her father when she was frustrated by the fact that the fish were not biting.

His advice had been for her to relax and think about something that made her happy. Her thoughts would not necessarily make the fish bite but at least her time would have been spent being happy.

As soon as she had started thinking happy thoughts the fish began to bite.

She now jogged on the treadmill thinking about Matt and the kids that now called her Aunt.

She got off the treadmill totally soaked but with a smile on her face.

Sandra asked about the smile.

Alex explained and Sandra commented that every time she was with her she learned something valuable.

They took the elevator to the sixth floor and when they came around the corner and looked to the end to where the chair Alex had positioned was exactly as she had left they walked with some confidence toward it.

Alex reached into her bag to retrieve her keys and made sure her gun was in an easy to get to position. She went in and put the cookies into the oven

The next morning when she got ready to go out, she was surprised to find Sandra at her door.

She asked if she had been there all night and was relieved to learn the Sandra had been replaced shortly after getting the warm cookies.

Alex asked whether Sandra was ready for some light shopping and maybe a quick sandwich for lunch.

Sandra said that she was to do whatever Alex wanted.

Alex went to the mall to a bookstore to get a book for each of the kids that called her Aunt. Nolan was Trey and Lesley's son, and Linda and Lorie were the daughters of Annie the woman that Alex had rescued from being held captive by her kidnapper for fifteen years.

Buying the books went quicker than planned.

She decided to eat something Asian and went to a Thai restaurant in Blue Ash. When she pulled into the parking lot, a car with a blue strip down its side immediately caught her eye.

Alex knew immediately that it was the same blue as that of the attack pickup. There were several restaurants within a few moments' walk. She walked over to the car and examined the paint. It was new and had recently been put on the car. She took out her knife and took a sample where the paint went into the wheel well.

She put the sample into a zip lock bag that she had in her car.

She knew that she would need to wait until the owner came back to the car. She needed to see who that person was and then determine how long they had owned the car.

Alex looked over to Sandra and told her to think happy thoughts. They were fishing.

Sandra smiled and asked if that made her a partner versus a guard.

Alex smiled and replied that she was pleased to have her as a partner.

About twenty minutes later a woman returned to her car.

Alex approached her and showed her badge. She explained that she was interested in the car and wondered how long the woman, who had identified herself as Marge, had owned the car.

Marge said that it was only the second day that she had owned it and that it had not yet been registered in her name, but she had the paperwork to prove it was hers.

Alex asked if Marge would let her take pictures of the paperwork.

She was certain that the title would lead to the person who had painted on the stripe and perhaps to the person responsible for the attack on her.

The Chief heard Mary-Anne answer his phone. He enjoyed the energy increase in her voice as she said hello to Alex, but he immediately knew that there was some sort of important information about the shooting that happened the day before.

He put down the book he had been reading and walked toward the entry area where he had left his phone.

Mary-Anne handed him the phone. He gave her a peck and thanked her then he turned his attention to Alex.

He always had this feeling that Alex was his daughter. He kept that to himself, but he worried about her like she was one. He knew she was the toughest person that he had ever worked with, but she was not invincible.

The excitement in her voice had him immediately at attention.

Alex had found a person who had bought a car that had a blue stripe painted down its side. The sample of paint from the car was a perfect match to the paint on the pickup.

The person now driving the car had the registration paper and had written a check to buy the car and she had told her where she had bought the car.

Alex told him they had the painter of the pickup.

Alex asked if she should arrest him or bring him in for questioning.

The Chief replied that he would call on Bill and Travis to bring the person in for questioning. She should continue doing whatever she planned for the day.

He would keep her in the loop

After hanging up he looked up Bill's number and gave him a call. He learned that Trevor had gone to Lake Cumberland and was at least four hours away.

The Chief asked Bill if the two of them could be partners and go see the fellow who had painted the pickup and a blue stripe on the car that Alex had found.

The drive to Oxford took him through his early study of the Ku Klux Klan and its strong showing in Ohio.

He asked Bill what he knew about the Klan's presence in Ohio.

He was not surprised to hear Bill say that he thought the Klan was located in Mississippi or Alabama.

He shared with Bill that at its height, the Klan had elected several Senators and Representatives to Congress

He made the point that at that time the Klan's headquarters was just north of Oxford Ohio.

He went on to point out that Alex's attackers location made this a possible racist hate crime.

He took the time to point out that the Klan had done a million person march on Washington around 1947.

This was long before Martin Luther King suggested a similar march to make the point for civil rights. In fact, given his knowledge of history, King had most likely known about the Clan's march and had tailored his message as a counter to that march.

He laughed when Bill called him professor and asked if there was a quiz when they got to Miami University.

The address on the registration turned out to be bogus. The address the new owner had given for where the car was purchased put them in front of a storage facility.

The Chief got on the phone and called the owner of the storage facility. The gate rolled open and the Chief drove his car into the parking area.

He asked about the dumpster that was at the end of the parking area and found out that it was scheduled for pickup on the following Tuesday.

He looked at Bill, gave a small chuckle and said there was no quiz but there was dumpster duty and pointed to it.

Bill gave a groan as he walked toward the dumpster.

He followed the owner into the office.

He asked if he had ever seen a bright blue pickup and was rewarded with a yes.

When he asked about a name and address of the owner, he was asked if a search warrant was needed.

He looked at the owner of the facility and said that if that was a request then he would get the paperwork but that the storage facility would be under lock and key until he got the paperwork.

The owner held up his hand and said he would show him the rental unit where the blue pickup had been stored. He also let the chief know about a car that had been parked out front with a blue stripe for most of a day before it was sold or at least moved before he could complain about it.

As they walked to the garage unit, he saw Bill hold up two large black bags.

The smell of fresh paint permeated the air as the door to the unit went up.

He asked the owner for the name and address of the person renting the unit.

He called dispatch with the address and found that it too was a fake.

He decided to call the local police and get them on board in the search for the home of the owner of the blue pickup.

He and Bill would take the two trash bags and make sure it was a match to the blue paint on the pickup.

He was convinced that the key break in the case had occurred.

Alex's keen observation skills and immediate follow up had connected a car in Cincinnati to a storage facility north of Oxford.

He asked Bill to come back to the facility and stake it out for the rest of the weekend.

8 Hate

Trey enjoyed his spacious backyard. He had put up a tall privacy fence around it. He had gates out to each neighbor and often had them in for a cookout. He liked the privacy fence so he could feel more at ease when he was out playing with Nolan.

He was looking forward to the backyard barbeque. He was having Alex over and because of the attack on her she would be accompanied by Sandra assigned to guard her.

Sandra was becoming a person who the family knew and considered a friend.

Annie and her two girls would also be part of the crowd. The two girls had become regular visitors and spend quite a bit of time with Nolan.

All three of the kids called Alex, "Aunt Alex."

Trey knew that Alex loved that title.

He was glad that the kids had taken a great liking to her and Matt.

The days had been hot so he figured that the activities would begin in the backyard but would probably end up in the house, with the kids playing down in the basement. The adults would be in the kitchen and the family room.

This was the third get together since the formal dinner that they had hosted that had ended in a gun battle in his house between Alex and several intruding attackers.

Their guns were silenced by Alex's display of her capabilities as she shot the intruder coming in by the front door with her service revolver that she held in her right hand. She almost simultaneously shot the intruder coming in through the back door and the kitchen with a three-fifty-seven revolver in her left hand while it was still in her purse.

He had marveled at her readiness and her immediate cool and swift response. He watched as she dropped her weapons and scooped up the kids and got them out of the family room and into the master bedroom. There was a dead man in the kitchen with the back of his head blow off and one laying in the foyer hallway with a gaping hole out his right forehead.

Alex had the kids in the master bedroom playing chutes and ladders and eating ice cream.

The Chief had taken control and demanded to know how the two thugs could have gotten past the security that was supposed to surround the house.

That case was directly involve with the Mexican drug cartels. It had sent him to the hospital for more than two weeks with two broken ribs a dislocated shoulder and a concussion caused by multiple kicks to his head.

Alex had saved him and had eliminated all but one of the thugs that had injured him. He came to realize how deadly she could be when attacked.

He was certain that she had shot the surviving thug in the leg to make him reveal the next boss up the food chain.

She had sought out that boss, his boss and had gone up the chain of drug bosses until she reached the very top.

None survived her confrontation.

She shared that she had given each a chance to be arrested and their response was to try to shoot her.

They had underestimated her resolute intent and her ability with a gun and her willingness to pull the trigger.

He rolled the grill to the platform he had built for it.

He looked proudly around the yard. The swing set with the attached playhouse beneath the large maple tree was a gift from Alex.

Nolan and the two girls loved to play there. It was in the shade of the tree and was usually at least ten degrees cooler than the rest of the yard.

Unfortunately, the picnic table did not have a similar sized tree. He had set up a canopy to shade it but somehow it always seemed hotter beneath the canopy.

He did a quick second tour to make sure everything was ready and then proceeded to go back into the house.

He took in the kitchen pull down container mounted arm's length above his head that held his weapon. He had put up a similar container in every room. It had a pull down latch that needed a strong twist to open but one that was easy for him. This had been Alex's idea of child proofing his weapon. She had also suggested having two loaded cartridge cases that could quickly be put into the weapon.

He chuckled to himself as he remembered Alex saying that Matt wanted her to quit sleeping with her gun and to do the same thing in her apartment.

Matt had said that he did not want to be the victim of one of her nightmares.

Trey had made two containers and had given them to her.

She had thanked him and let him know that they had been mounted and that she needed a stool to stand on to reach them. She had wanted them high enough to keep the kids from being able to reach them.

Lesley and Nolan were not yet back from a last minute run to the grocery, so the house was quiet. He poured himself a glass of iced tea, squeezed in some lemon juice and sat down at the kitchen table.

The doorbell rang and he went cautiously to see who it was.

He saw Alex and Sandra and opened the door.

After the hello's he invited them into the kitchen for a glass of iced tea.

Alex shared the fact that Sandra and she had found a car with a blue strip on it that matched the paint job on the pickup of the shooter. The Chief and Bob had tracked the car down to a storage unit north of Oxford and were on the trail of the person who had painted the truck.

Trey asked if he should invite the Chief and Bob to the barbeque. He smiled at Alex's response that it would be the fastest way to find out what the two knew.

Trey put in a call to each. Bob replied that he was on surveillance for the weekend and couldn't make it. The Chief accepted and asked if it was OK to bring the boss.

Trey replied that bosses always got their way

After the call he asked Alex if she had any clue as to why she had been attacked, he was surprised at the answer.

He listened as she explained that the location of where the pickup had been painted suggested that it could be as simple as hate.

He shook his head and made the point that he did not understand such an extreme point of view that would lead a person to do such a thing.

He also made the point that most people having that point of view did not target police detectives and that the person they were dealing with must not be very stable or might be angered by her successes

Alex said that she was not sure. She excused herself and said that she was going back to her apartment to relax.

She asked Trey to hold her gifts for the kids. She was excited about the barbeque and planned to come early so she and Matt could play with the kids before everyone arrived.

She and Sandra got up and went to the car.

When they arrived at the apartment Alex asked if Sandra wanted to come in.

Sandra declined and said that the Chief had made it clear the last time that her position was outside of the apartment.

Alex nodded in agreement and promised a BLT for dinner.

She closed the door and was just about to change into some running clothes when the apartment doorbell rang.

Matt was standing outside of her door with a smile on his face. His green eyes once again made her heart take an extra beat.

She pulled him into the room and her embrace. She asked him to join her in the gym and promised a BLT sandwich dinner afterwards.

She smiled when he said sure, but that desert had to be special.

9 *Under the Overpass*

Paul had rented a space in the park where he could safely spend the night. He slept in the back of his pickup. He had loaded the stuff that he felt would be most useful. The back seat was packed. He had previously outfitted his pickup so he could go hunting and stay anywhere in the woods and be comfortable. The bed was up above the cab. There was a small sink and stove on one side and a bench on the other side. The gun rack was above the bench. He had a scoped 308 and several small caliber rifles for small game and a shotgun for hunting quail and pheasants.

He figured he might be able to salvage the rest of his personal property by putting his dumb cousin into business and selling him the acreage. That would have to wait until he was safely down in Mississippi. Once he was situated and things cooled down he would worry about those kinds of things. For now, he wanted to get on with the show and then get out of town.

He had arranged to meet his two Mississippi supporters at the location that he felt would be the most likely point to shoot and kill his target.

He had spent a lot of time watching which way she normally chose to go. Sunday's seemed to be a drive north on seventy one.

He figured she went shopping at the Kenwood Mall. She normally drove an older Ford police issue automobile. This gave him the impression that she was at the bottom of the totem pole in the organization.

The meeting place was a business parking lot.

It was a Sunday, so the lot was empty.

They parked in the back to be out of sight.

They discussed how they planned to shoot and kill their target.

He drew the job to look out for the car that would be the target. He walked out on the overpass and watched the cars coming up the north bound entrance ramp.

He had walked the overpass many times as he waited for the car. He was beginning to think that he had miscalculated then he spotted the car entering the highway. He pointed it out to the shooters.

The two from Mississippi went down under the overpass.

He continued walking back across the bridge as he watched the car approach.

He had expected the roar of the gunfire, but the shooters had silencers on their rifles.

As he walked across he saw multiple holes puncture the front window of the car. He figured the job was done but the car disappeared below the overpass.

He listened as he anticipated his two conspirators to finish the job. Instead, he heard the rapid fire of a revolver and then silence.

He had been about to go see the carnage but immediately turned and ran as fast as he could for his pickup. When he got to the corner of the building and looked back there was some smoke coming up from under the overpass, but the two shooters were nowhere in sight.

He got into his pickup and slowly left the parking lot and drove at the speed limit toward the west side of town.

He figured he would find out the details by listening to the news.

The evening before, Alex had made the promised BLT for the three of them.

Sandra's replacement had shown up early and earned one as well.

Afterwards, Sandra had excused herself so she could be back on time to take up her guard duty in the morning.

The next morning had been ham and eggs and then some time relaxing on the veranda and doing some reading.

She and Matt both wanted to get to the barbeque early and did not plan on having any lunch. Matt had volunteered to drive his SUV, but Alex had declined.

She felt that her official police vehicle should be used.

She was having one of her premonitions and insisted that all three of them wear bullet proof Kevlar vests.

Matt put up a small objection but gave in when Alex said it was the condition for him to ride in her car.

She said he could choose to drive by himself in his SUV.

He said that he was going with her and put on the Kevlar vest that she handed him.

Alex led the way to the car. Once everyone was strapped in she head out toward US 71 north.

She was just speeding up the merge ramp when the bullets began to rip through the front window. She stomped down on the accelerator and felt the car surge as she turned the wheel and ran the car up the cement slope under the overpass. The front slammed into the cement sloped base and the front windshield collapsed inward.

Trey watched as smoke bellowed from under the hood.

Alex leaped through the open window and rolled up and over the hood. She felt the bullets hit her vest but concentrated on finding her target.

The shooter that was visible was wearing a helmet. Her first shot was through his neck and the second was just above the bullet proof vest he was wearing.

The second shooter stepped out with his rifle with a bump stock that made it into in a rapid fire action. He met the same fate, but his bullets did hit Alex and took her breath away.

She continued her assault until she was sure her attackers were down.

She looked over to where Sandy was passed out and Matt was checking her pulse.

She kept her eyes on the two shooters. She walked over and made sure they were dead.

She struggled to walk up the slope to the street above.

There was no one in sight.

As she went back to the car she looked down at her vest and realized that she had been hit three times in the chest and knew that she had taken several more in back.

She realized that she had blood running down on the back of her neck.

She looked at Matt and asked if he was alright. He was attending to Sandy. She too had been hit three times in the chest.

Matt looked out at the entrance ramp and saw an EMT vehicle and flagged them over.

Sandy came awake and looked at Alex and asked if she had pulled off another miracle.

Alex joked back that she left miracles to Johnnie and that she dealt in lead and death.

She pointed to the attackers to emphasize her last statement.

Matt took some ribbing from the EMT team that had responded because it was his team.

Alex let the EMT team examine her. The blood on her neck came from a small scratch she had somehow received when she went through the front window of the car.

Once she was checked out she went to talk to the senior highway patrol that was managing the shooting site. She suggested that several officers should see if there was a vehicle behind the office building on the street above.

He looked at her badge and then at her and asked if he should contact her boss and if she needed a ride somewhere.

Alex thanked him and told him that she had been on the way to a barbeque where she would see her boss. And that she needed a ride back to her apartment.

She went back to where Sandra was sitting on the bumper of the EMT unit having a small argument with the team leader.

She listened for a moment to Sandy's objection of being taken to the hospital. She then held up her Kevlar vest to show the EMT members that she too had taken three hits in the chest and then she showed him the hits on the side and back of her vest. She said that she was functioning just fine. She assured them that Matt would make sure they took their pain pills later in the day and then the next day.

She then took Sandy's hand and led her away. She looked at Matt and asked him if the ride he had suggested earlier was still available.

10 Barbeque

They were the last to arrive at the barbeque. Lindsey greeted them at the front door. She said everyone was in the backyard and the talk was all about the shooting under the overpass.

She shared the fact the Chief had received a call and had been very animated about the shooting. He was still brooding about the attack. He kept saying that he was going to trace the two shooters back to their home location and make sure their friends felt the heat.

Alex followed Lindsey out to the back yard and got hugs from Nolan, Linda, and Lorie. She gave each of them the gift that she had brought them and then stood up as the Chief came forward.

She raised her hand and asked everyone to go back to eating barbeque and that she, Sandra, and Matt would each relate what had happened after they got their food and had a chance to take a bite.

She said that wanted a sip of a cold beer and a couple of ribs before she was willing to talk.

She pointed to Matt and said that he was the talkative one that should talk about what had happened.

Lindsey handed her a plate with a cob of corn, three ribs and some grilled vegetables.

She led her to the table.

Sandra sat down beside her and raised her beer and gave a toast, "to our own lead slinging Black Annie Oakley. She saved all of us."

Mary-Anne came over and gave Alex a hug and commented that she had seldom seen her other half so angry. She was worried he might do something rash.

Alex reassured her that she always caused the Chief to flare up but then he always put solid plans into action.

She explained that she and the Chief had come to an agreement about her getting the oldest car in the fleet because she had gone through at least one car on every case she had been on.

She figured that counting the car under the bridge, she had now destroyed five official department vehicles. Even if the vehicle under the bridge that survived it had bullet holes that needed filling and at least a new radiator and windshield needing replacement.

Alex listened as Matt recounted his experience. She was surprised by how he had experienced the attack.

He had immediately followed her command to get down.

He was surprised by the surge of the car as she gunned the engine and then ran the car up the cement apron under the bridge.

He said in doing so she took out a wire fence and when she stopped shooting and he got out of the car he realized that Alex had silenced the shooters. The car frame was bent, and the doors would not open. He forced the passenger seat back and got Sandy out of the car. She had passed out after being hit by three bullets in the chest.

He related that to him it seemed that the firing was almost continuous and endless.

When he watched Alex turn over her weapon to the Highway Patrol, he realized that she had only shot four times.

The rest of the gunfire had been from the two shooters.

He commented that the shooters had on protective face shields and helmets and bullet proof vests. Alex had shot them under the chin and through the throat.

He was amazed that under the duress of being hit by their shooting she had calmly shot each of her attackers in the only possible place that would have the desired outcome.

The Chief came over and sat across from her.

He looked at her and then at Sandra. "I am not sure I can assign anyone to protect you. You seem to get them shot. And how am I going to explain needing another car?"

Alex smiled at him and replied that, "It was his problem and all she was thinking about was how good the ribs that Trey had prepare tasted."

She finished with, " I love you too."

And got up to get another helping.

The Chief looked over at Sandra and asked how she was feeling.

Sandy replied that she was already feeling the pain and she had taken half the hits that Alex had. She figured that she had to suck it up if she was going to keep up with the person she was supposed to be guarding.

She went on to say that it seemed that Alex was always the one saving her versus her saving Alex.

Trey looked at Alex coming toward the grill. He knew she would be hurting by morning.

She was tough but she had taken at least seven hits.

He was not surprised at her having put on the Kevlar vests and making her passengers do the same.

He knew that she was always attentive to her premonitions and caution was a habit she had developed.

He was not surprised by her insistence of coming to the barbeque.

She loved to get her hugs from Nolan, Linda, and Lorie.

Also, he was not surprised at her getting Matt to relate the events of the attack.

He knew his partner well enough that she wanted time to process the attacks that had happened to her and time to figure out why and how to stop any future attacks.

He pointed to the barbequed ribs, chicken, and vegetables.

He nodded when Alex asked if he would sit with her at the kitchen table.

He led the way in.

Alex sat down and asked if Trey had a glass of iced tea she could have. He nodded and opened the frig and got a glass from the cupboard. He filled it with ice and poured the tea.

Alex commented that she seemed to be a magnet for shooters and people trying to kill her. She went on and pointed out that she would be on desk duty for at least two weeks.

Then she made the point that Trey had been a super partner but if he wanted to become lead on his own team she would understand.

Trey looked at her and asked if she was joking.

He pointed out that she had saved his life in two ways.

First she had pulled him out of his PTSD like depression, had given him purpose and then she had physically risked her life to save him in the drug case.

He figured to be her partner for as long as he worked as a detective.

Alex beamed a smile and thanked him for his support.

She said she was going to need it by morning when all the pain from her bruises would be spiking.

She added that she would be in the office to dig into the case and to be in a safe spot where she could relax.

She went on and said that the two weeks of mandatory desk duty was going to be focused on finding the person who had orchestrated two attempts to kill her.

She was not going to allow this person the latitude to try it again.

She was taking the battle to wherever he might be.

Her phone rang and she recognized the gong as her father calling.

She looked at Trey and commented that the news must have picked up the shooting and it must have made the Chicago area news.

Her father came on and asked if she were OK. The news had shown the condition of her car. They had withheld her name, but she was the only black female detective on the Cincinnati Detective Unit.

He then said that she should come home so they could go fishing and that it was not a request. She could invite as many people as she wished but she had better be at home by Tuesday because he had taken the week off to go fishing with her.

Alex had kept her phone on the speaker mode. She looked over at Trey and asked if he wanted to take his family to go fishing. She made the point that she planned to invite Matt.

Trey looked at her and smiled and replied that it would be a great vacation and he was sure the Lindsey and Nolan would enjoy it as well.

Alex walked out into the back yard and announced that her parents had just invited everyone to come to her home north of Chicago for a summer fishing and pool side extravaganza vacation.

She asked for a show of hands of who wanted to take him up on his offer to take them fishing. She gave a small laugh when everyone raised their hands.

She then replied to her father and informed him that every room in their house would in use. She would let him know the exact number of people at the end of the day.

Alex then gave her love to him and to her mom and hung up.

She then looked at Trey and pointed to the backyard.

Let's enjoy ourselves while the sun shines.

11 Chicago

Rose-Anne looked at Russel and asked if they had just invited the entire Cincinnati detective unit to vacation at their house.

Russel looked at her and replied that Alex was her daughter and as always projected her extremes. He was just a quiet fisherman seeking a fishing partner and he figured it was all her fault for suggesting he call Alex

Rose-Anne laughed and replied that he was going to need a bigger boat or maybe several. She then asked when he had arranged to take vacation.

Russel smiled replied that it would happen tomorrow. He went on to defend his small lie by reminding her that she had insisted he get Alex to come home. He said she should reward him for being successful

He then reminded Rose-Anne that Alex's last time going out fishing on the lake had ended up with a coal freighter on fire and the crew dead.

The two of them had been apprehended by the DEA and scanned for transmitters and that they found two transmitters on Alex at different times during that trip.

He wondered what excitement would follow Alex home this time.

Rose-Anne laughed at Russel's description of the last time Alex visited.

She pointed out that they had been able to meet and interact with Matt and that he seemed to be the perfect partner for Alex.

She also pointed out that Alex had learned about crime scene investigation from her favorite Northern University college professor.

She finished the reminder with the great family fishing trip they had all made and the picnic that followed.

She said that she would take some time off as well and would arrange to have their meals catered and the bill sent to him. She suggested either renting a big yacht or several fishing boats.

Back at Trey's, Annie approached Alex and asked if the invitation was real and if so, she wanted to go, the two girls had immediately told her to make sure that they got to go to Aunt Alex's home.

Alex smiled and nodded that it was a real invitation and that the three would share the same room at her parents' home.

Lindsey was in the process of getting everyone to come into the house and get away from the mosquitos when Alex let her know that she needed to get home and under a hot shower.

Alex walked over to Matt and let him know that she needed to go home. She looked at Sandra and asked whether she would like to stay for the night at her apartment. The second bedroom was available, and it had its own shower.

The Chief had overheard her and made the point that both of them had the coming week off. He would be assigning another person to be guarding the apartment and then personally guarding her during the day.

He jokingly asked that Alex refrain from getting any more of her guards shot.

Trey walked her to the door and thanked her for the invitation to go fishing and that Nolan was super excited about it.

Alex smiled at Trey and simply said, "For every grey cloud, there is a silver lining."

Once back to the apartment, Matt stopped at the front door and had to guide Alex and Sandra, through the crowd of news people and camera personnel, to the apartment entrance. It seemed that the media had figured out that there was only one black female detective in the Cincinnati Detective unit.

Alex thanked him and led the way to the elevator.

Once in the apartment she broke out the bottle of over-the-counter pain medication and offered it to Sandy. She took two of the extra strength and said she was going for a hot shower.

After a good twenty minutes under the hot water, she dried off and looked in the mirror.

She laughed at the memory of her snide remark to the white EMT nurse about how hard it was to see a bruise when your skin was black.

Now she was looking at her bruised spots and realized how true that statement had been.

She might not be able to see them very well, but she could feel every spot where she had been hit.

She had no trouble falling asleep as she lay against Matt. He had his arm around her and gave her a good night kiss.

The next morning, she woke up and realized that she barely remembered Matt getting into bed and she was now the only person in it.

She got up, very sore but ready for the day. At least as ready as she could.

The bruises were now making themselves felt.

Matt walked in with a breakfast tray and was surprised to see her dressed.

He turned and walked out ahead of her and put the tray on the only table in the apartment. He said that he was going to make two waffles and two eggs for himself and would join her for breakfast.

Alex took the seat that allowed her to watch Matt prepare the waffles and fry the two eggs.

He had adopted her favorite way to eat waffles and eggs. Plenty of syrup and butter between the waffles and the two over easy eggs on top. This worked with both waffles and pancakes.

She only ate this combination on weekends.

She slowly sipped her coffee and enjoyed waking up. She took two more pills.

Matt had just finished and brought his plate to the table when the doorbell rang.

Alex held up her hand and walked to the front door. She positioned her stool so she could look out of the peep hole but be off to the side.

A smile brightened her face as she opened the door and greeted Johnnie. She took note of the guard sitting on the chair that Sandy had brought. She politely said good morning and then pulled Johnnie in and closed the door.

Johnnie pointed at the clock and made the point that it was nine o'clock. He went on to say that he had made some initial reservations for flights to Chicago, and he wanted to make sure they fit Alex's desire. He had volunteered to arrange travel for everyone that had accepted the invitation to go to her house for vacation.

He asked if it was Ok if he brought his significant other and if so there would be twelve people that needed beds or a place to sleep. The Chief suggested that they plan on the family with young kids staying at your place but that the rest of the folks should find a close by hotel.

Johnnie went on to say that it put Trey and his family in one room, Annie and her two daughters in another room and she and Matt in her room. He looked at her and asked whether she was OK with the arrangement so far.

He had talked with Alex's mother and had obtained the name of a nearby hotel. Everything was set and awaiting approval.

Alex looked at Johnnie and simply said, "as always, my miracle worker."

Sandra walked in and asked if she were interrupting anything, asked about coffee and about two more pain pills. She made the comment that her three bruises looked terrible.

Alex smiled and said that hers didn't show up at all.

Matt pointed to his plate and said that she was just in time for her breakfast.

He got up and went to the stove to make another breakfast. He smiled as he thought that he needed to be as determined about breakfast as Alex was about solving her cases as he put the pancake dough into the skillet.

<u>12 Fishing on the Lake</u>

*A*lex called her previous taxi driver and arranged for him to pick she and Matt up at the airport. The flight was uneventful and the ride to her home was relaxing.

She and Matt chatted and conjectured about the shooting attempts that had occurred. Matt made the point that someone had fixated on killing her. He commented that from the first day they had met he had watched her take out her adversaries and he figured she would do it again.

Alex thanked him for his confidence but pointed out that so far she had been lucky, but she had no clue on how to hunt down her current adversary because there seemed to be no motive other than perhaps an overwhelming hate on the part of the perpetrator's part.

She pointed out that she had gotten a break by spotting the car with the blue strip.

She figured she got that break with the help of a hand from above.

The drive down the tree covered lane up to the house seemed to signal a quiet weekend and seeing her mother and father coming out to the circle to greet them brought a sense of relief to her.

Matt paid the taxi driver and joined her in getting hugs and being led into the house.

Not long after, Trey and his family arrived. Trey had previously been at her parents' home so when the tour of the house began he excused himself and walked out to the pool side where Matt and her father were sitting and talking.

Alex held Nolan's hand and followed behind her mother and Lyndsey for the tour of the house. She had to explain to Nolan that she was not rich, but she agreed that her parents were rich.

Lindsey commented that the bedroom that she and her family were sleeping in was bigger than the combined space of the three bedrooms at her house.

Alex suggested that Nolan get his swimsuit on and take an evening dip in the pool.

She then excused herself and went down to the pool area and joined Matt, Trey, and her father.

Trey handed her a paper with the flight numbers and times that each of the others would be arriving.

Alex noted that most of them would arrive on the morning flights that arrived within a few minutes of each other. She arrange for a van to pick up the bulk of those coming.

She sent her taxi driver to pick up Annie, and her two daughters.

Johnnie would arrive at one. He and Mary would meet in Chicago.

She arranged for her taxi driver to pick them up.

She then sent messages to each person and let them know about the arrangements.

It was not long after that Nolan came out into the pool area. He was about to jump in when her father stopped him and explained the rules about swimming in the pool.

Then for the rest of the evening they all sat and made small talk.

The next morning Alex sat on the edge of her bed and tried to shake off the feeling of helplessness that she had fought with all night long.

Matt asked if she was OK and mentioned that she had tossed and turned and mumbled for most of the night. She took his hand and thanked him for holding her and that she remembered the kisses to her forehead.

She then stood up and went into the shower where she let the hot water flow over her head and down her body. She was not sure how long she had been in the shower but when she got out she saw a note from Matt that the smell of coffee had pulled him to the kitchen.

Alex came down the back steps into the kitchen where she found her mother and Matt sitting and enjoying a cup of coffee and toast.

She asked if there was a chance of having one of those delicious grilled cheese sandwiches that she had so enjoyed as a young girl.

Her mother laughed and replied that to her she was still her young girl and that the grilled cheese would be done in a flash.

She asked Matt if he wanted one and then declared that it would be three grilled cheese.

Alex was just sitting down when her father came in and asked if he could join them in a grilled cheese sandwich as well.

Alex stood up and said that she would help get things set up and that she would leave the grilling to her mother.

Trey, Lindsey, and Nolan came in as her mother was in the middle of preparing the grilled cheese sandwiches.

She asked who wanted grilled cheese sandwiches and if anyone wanted eggs to go with the sandwich.

She took out a frying pan to fry the eggs for her father and Trey.

After breakfast Alex asked if anyone wanted to go for a walk along the beach.

Nolan immediately said yes but it was clear to Alex that neither Trey, nor Lyndsey was very interested.

She suggested that the beach walk should wait until Linda and Lorie arrived. Then she would take the three for a walk along the beach.

When Annie arrived with Linda and Lorie, Nolan excitedly led them up the stairs to show them their bedroom.

Alex joined her mother in guiding Annie into the family room and then out to the pool area where everyone was sitting and relaxing.

Nolan, Linda, and Lorie came out to the pool area dressed in their swim trunks and declared they were ready for a walk along the beach.

Alex let Annie know that she had promised to take the kids for a walk along the beach. She looked at Matt to see if he was willing. He stood up and declared that he wanted to take a walk along the beach.

Alex knew that lunch was to be self-help sandwiches and that dinner would be Surf and Turf with the entire list of guests.

She made the point that she and Matt would treat the kids to a surprise lunch and that they would be back in time to get ready for dinner.

She then led the three kids out to the garage where her Jaguar was parked.

She put the top down.

Then got the three situated and seat belted and then slowly backed out of the garage. The kids waved at Lindsey and Annie who had come out to see their brood off.

The walk along the beach was a welcome relief for Alex.

She and Matt walked hand in hand and watched as the three kids frolicked in the shallows and enjoyed the small waves that washed in.

Alex knew that though the breeze kept everyone cool the sun hit with all of its force.

After a short time, she enticed the three kids by offering to take them for a sandwich, fries, and an ice cream for desert.

She and Matt skipped lunch. They had both decided to save their stomachs for the Surf and Turf dinner that was being catered by one of her mother's Chef buddies.

Her mother had paid for the food, but her Chef buddy did not want compensation but wanted to have pictures with Alex and get her opinion on how well he had prepared the food.

He added that he wanted to use the pictures as a draw on his cooking podcast

Alex had agreed to the arrangement but was surprised at the fact that a professional photography team had a list of the various scenes they planned to have her in. They had scripted various scenes and asked her to don various outfits. She went from being dressed to look like she was going swimming, to being in her professional work outfit. When the film crew learned she was called Aunt by the kids, they wanted a shot where she was sitting at the small table where the three were having their dinner.

The constant turnover of Alex posing with each of the guests more or less ruined the dinner that her mother had wanted to enjoy.

Alex apologized about the constant interruption and was happy when her mother asked her friend to stop the advertising and to focus on pleasing the dinner guests.

Alex enjoyed the haddock's a unique and delicious flavor that the coconut and turmeric sauce gave it. The dollar sized filet mignon with a dollop of brie and sautéed in garlic butter was out of this world and Alex closed her eyes and enjoyed each bite.

She was joined by everyone when she raised her alcohol free wine and proposed a toast to one of the best meals she had ever eaten.

Not long after Alex announced that she was headed to bed and would see everyone on the boat in the morning. She reminded everyone that the boat was to leave the peer by seven. She announced that she would be serving breakfast by six am.

Early in the dark of the next morning she backed her Jag out of the garage and drove slowly to the dock where the boat would be located. Matt sat quietly with his eyes closed as they drove to the harbor area. He had stayed up later than Alex and was not yet ready to be awake.

She parked in what she considered her normal spot that was under the lamp pole at the end of the parking lot. This was the closest spot to the pier.

Alex got out and after Matt closed his door she locked the Jag and walked toward the bait and tackle shop.

She took in the fact that the gate to the pier was locked and continued to the shop.

Dexter, the owner of the dock area usually opened up early in the morning and then turned the shop over to one of several people who worked for him.

Alex opened the door, waved to Dexter, and walked over to the counter where he was drinking a cup of coffee.

He commented that she was early and that he had not unlocked the gate to the dock.

She agreed with the early part and said that she had breakfast duty and was going to get the coffee and the cooking area ready.

She and Matt followed Dexter. Once the gate was opened, Alex asked if he wanted breakfast and that he could be one of her first customers.

Dexter said that he would not be able to leave the shop until well after the Golden Goose left with all the people that would be fishing.

Matt asked about the name of the yacht and was told that Dexter had given it that name because it was the one thing that he had purchase for himself and his family that was strictly for recreation. This was the first time he had let someone rent it. He had done so because for as long as he could remember, Alex and her father had been loyal customers.

He commented that Alex's father had moored his boat in the harbor for at least twenty-five years. He had also provided enough fish that Dexter figured he had added a significant chunk of extra change to his business.

Alex led the way down the pier. She commented that on weekends the pier had around forty fishing boats lining both sides.

She boarded and began to get the galley ready for her to prepare breakfast. Matt found the coffee pot and prepared a full pot of coffee.

She could see her parents accompanied by everyone staying in the house get out of the van parked next to her car. She made sure the pancakes were cooking and then she went out to the pier to greet everyone.

She hugged the three kids and let them know that the pancakes, syrup, and eggs were ready for them.

She watched a person walk across the end of the pier and go into the bait shop.

It was too dark for her to see his face.

She figured he was the one who had rented the boat tied across from the yacht.

Breakfast was in full swing when the van bringing the rest of the folks who had been in the hotel arrived.

Alex watched as her father greeted them and got them all aboard. As soon as everyone was on, he had Trey and Matt release the ropes from the pier and jumped back on board.

The trip out to the fishing area would take about an hour. This gave Alex time to finish serving breakfast and everyone to take their time eating.

She thanked Mary, Lindsey, and Annie for helping clean up.

She took a moment to step out on deck.

As she looked back toward the shore she thought she saw a boat following.

She went back to get the binoculars and then looked back to where she thought she had seen the boat.

There was nothing.

She attributed her reaction to the experience on the last case. She had almost been blown out of the water by the helicopter gunship that had pursued her and caused her to board the coal freighter that turned out to be the ship the helicopter had been launched from. She had shot down the helicopter that crashed into the coal barge and set it on fire.

She had killed the entire crew as they pursued her in a rubber raft while one of them shot at her. She had watched the burning coal barge and the tug pushing it as it burned and eventually sunk.

She turned and listened as her father was getting everyone ready to fish.

She saw that Matt was at the helm and walked over to him. She gave him a hug and said that she was going to make the rounds before starting to fish.

Once she visited with Nolan and Trey and went to see how Linda and Lorrie were doing, she went up to the bow and put in her own pole.

She could not relax and continued to have an uneasy feeling.

It was an appropriate feeling that would have her ready for immediate action in the immediate future.

13 Closing the Circle

Paul arrived at his buddy's marina late in the afternoon. Going there had been more or less a serendipitous decision. He planned to go to Mississippi but figured going there directly would make it too easy for the law to catch him.

As he arrived and drove in, he was surprised at how affluent his friend had become. He could not believe that the quiet and shy person that Felix had been in school had been able to buy and establish the facility that now boasted two docks and hosted what seemed like more than a hundred yachts of various sizes.

He parked his pickup next to a big boat storage building that housed boats that various owners kept at the marina. As he walked up to the main office he walked by the pier that had the largest yacht in the harbor tied off. Its name, The Golden Goose was painted neatly on the bow in gold lettering.

Felix was surprised to see him and they greeted each other as old friends.

Paul complimented Felix on his success and asked if the Golden Goose was his boat.

Felix said that it was and that he was getting it ready to go out in the morning with a fishing party.

Felix asked if Paul wanted to go fishing and offered to let him use a boat for free. Paul readily accepted and agreed that he would pay for the live bait. He asked about plugging his camper into power and learned that there was an outlet at each parking space.

When he asked who was going out fishing on the Golden Goose he was shocked when Felix said that it was a longtime friend Professor Russel Evercrest and a party that his daughter had invited to go out.

The name Evercrest sent alarm bells off in his head. He asked if the professor was black and when that was confirmed Paul almost ran out of the bait shop.

Then the phrase, "the hand of god" flashed in his mind.

He thanked Felix for giving him the opportunity to go fishing and that he would share his catch when he came in after catching a few the next morning.

He walked back to his pickup and got in the back. His first act was to plug into the electrical outlet. Then he made himself several sandwiches and put them in his frig.

He then loaded his AR-15 and put it aside. A plan on how to take out his target flashed in his mind.

The more he thought about it the better it seemed.

He knew that he had been guided to his friend for a reason. He could not believe his luck in having randomly chosen to drive north and then he remembered the marina.

Very early the next morning, he stood in the dark between the building and the front of his truck and took in the sight of the huge power cruiser. He looked at what seemed to be a ridiculously small boat moored opposite of the cruiser and tied off. He wanted to walk out and check out the boat but felt it was too much exposure. He would wait, watch and when the cruiser left he would go to his boat and follow it out at a discrete distance.

A food deliver truck arrived and unloaded what seemed to be a huge amount of food. It appeared to him that those going out fishing were going to enjoy a great day.

He wondered who all was going fishing.

He chuckled as he thought of the carnage he would most likely hurl their way and figured a few would catch more than fish.

He stood watching while he prepared his fishing pole lines the way that his buddy had suggested.

He was planning to fish with two poles. He laughed at the fact that he might catch fish that he would not be able to clean before he went zipping out of the parking lot.

He knew that once he attacked the yacht, he would need to get back to his truck and disappear.

He hoped that he would be successful in taking out the black detective and maybe even get some of her friends.

He watched as first the detective that he had learned was called Alex arrived with a tall rather handsome black friend.

They got Dexter to open the gate to the pier and walked out to the yacht holding hands. He would make sure to target the friend. He wanted to inflict as much carnage as he could among those who were willing to support her.

He continued to stand in the shadow of the building and watched as a van delivered a group of people. He figured that her mother and father and friends with kids were arriving.

The chatter and laughter made him smile. He had no desire to hurt any kids, but collateral damage would not cause him any concern.

He saw his target come out and hug the three kids and wave them into the kitchen area. All seemed quiet after the group made it down to the yacht and got on.

The group that had been inside came out and sat around on the deck.

He then watched as another van arrived and seven people got out and walked down the pier.

Three were white and four were black. It was clear to him that this was a group of liberal twerps.

Anyone getting hit by a stray bullet deserved it. It lightened his concern about collateral damage because it would all be good damage.

He watched as the yacht pulled away from the pier. He then took his poles and walked to the head of the pier and leaned them against the fence. He put his AR-15 on the ground and dropped a blanket over it.

He walked into the bait shop and got a dozen live minnows and the rest of the bait. He figured he would get some fishing in before attacking the yacht.

He walked back to the head of the pier and after two trips to his boat he had everything on board. He could see the yacht clear the very far buoy with a flashing light.

He untied the boat and put the bow in line with the red lighted buoy. He wanted to follow the yacht long enough to get the heading they were on. Once he had that he would swing away for a short time and then get on that heading. He would then stay just out of sight and do some fishing until he figured everyone on the yacht was focused on catching fish and he could zoom in and mow them down. He figured he might even take several passes and really dish out a rain of lead.

He tuned his radio to a country western station and enjoyed the sunrise breaking over the far horizon.

He threw out his two lines and was soon rewarded with two hits that turned out to be keepers. He knew then that it was going to be a very good day.

He felt that the circle was closing, and it was closing exactly as he wished it would.

He wished he had brought out a full six pack, but he decided that the ham sandwich and a beer was about the best lunch he had enjoyed for some time.

After eating his sandwich, he went out to locate the yacht. The sun had made its way to about a ten o'clock height when he spotted the yacht. He turned and went to a point where he could no longer see it. He arranged his AR-15 so he could hold the boat heading by leaning against the steering wheel and rest the body of the gun on the windshield rim.

He felt the circle was closing, and it was closing exactly as he wished it would.

He felt invigorated and ready to finish the job of taking out his target. He would make sure that the yacht would never make it back to shore by opening up the bow.

He was not smart enough to realize that the design of the yacht would, at the hands of an expert captain, not sink and that the expert markswoman on board would make his trip in not only miserable but would disable both he and his boat.

14 High Noon Attack

*A*lex had seen what she thought was a boat following the yacht but when she used the yacht's binoculars, she could not see it.

The hair on the back of her neck was tingling. She knew that she had no hair on the back of her neck and that the feeling was one that almost always made her do things that seemed unnecessary but that later saved her life.

She asked Matt if he had brought his weapon and when he said he had, she asked him to put it in the compartment by the helm. She walked over to Trey and asked if he had his weapon and asked him to put it in the same place that Matt had put his. She decided not to ask the chief or Bill and Trevor. She put her gun on so that it was in the middle of her back and pulled on a large t-shirt.

She told Matt that if she shouted out that they were being attacked he was responsible for clearing the port side of the yacht and that she would clear the starboard side and get everyone down in the galley area.

He looked at her and asked if she had one of her premonitions.

She nodded in the affirmative.

She cast her line but found it hard to be patient or to think positive thoughts.

Everyone was spread along the sides of the back two thirds of the yacht. Annie and her two were on the port side and Lindsey and Nolan were on the starboard side.

When she saw the boat speeding toward them she knew.

She dropped her pole and in the loudest voice she could muster she yelled for everyone to get into the kitchen area and lay down on the floor.

She rushed back and pushed Lindsey and Nolan toward the back and then pushed them into the center of the boat toward the galley.

She pulled her gun and began to fire at the figure that was leaning against the steering wheel of the oncoming boat as he fired his AR-15 in rapid succession.

She felt a bullet hit her left shoulder but continued to fire at the figure. She was sure she hit him several times because he started to zig zag as he went by.

His firing was erratic and did not seem to be hitting anything but the side of the yacht.

Alex emptied her weapon and was about to turn away when Matt handed her his three-fifty-seven. It packed a much more damaging wallop, but she had to adjust to its bigger drop over the range she was shooting.

She fired repeatedly as the boat continued its erratic zigzag retreat. She was rewarded by smoked coming out of the engine, but the boat continued to speed away.

Her father shouted that he had to get the boat moving because it was taking on water. If he did not get the bow up they would sink.

Alex looked at Trey and the Chief who had their guns out and were returning them to the lock box by the helm.

She smiled when each said that they always carried their weapons when she was around.

Her father had the boat going full speed toward the harbor. He announced that by lifting the bow he made less speed, but it had stopped the flooding in the engine compartment.

He called ahead to the harbor and asked that someone, with the equipment to plug the bullet holes, meet them at the pier. He said that he had multiple holes in the bow.

As her father brought the boat in the bow up manner until the very last moment.

As he approached the pier Alex spotted the diver standing next to Felix.

She saw where the shooter had run the boat up onto the loading ramp and someone was climbing out of the water.

Alex could see someone running up the boat ramp and then across the parking lot. She wanted to immediately jump onto the dock.

She took the bull horn and told the person by the loading ramp not to touch the boat that was sitting on the ramp.

She more quietly told the diver on the pier that most of the bullet holes would be on the starboard side.

She then turned to those on board and asked them to stay on board until she, Trey, the Chief and Bill and Trevor cleared the area.

She had tears of anger as she apologized for having put them all at risk and then jumped down to the pier. She was rushing up the pier toward the parking lot when she saw a black pickup with a camper pull out of the lot.

She pulled her gun but realized she did not have a clear shot. She was rushing for her car when Trey caught up with her and asked what she was doing.

She looked at him and stopped.

She had to get on her knees because she was dizzy, then she realized that she had blood dripping from her right hand fingertips and onto her gun.

A black DEA van stopped in front of her and one of the DEA team carried out a first aid kit.

Alex sat down on the curb and let them examine the wound. She had been hit once in the muscle between her neck and her collar bone. The shot had gone cleanly through and had not done much damage.

Harold Zimmerman came over to her. He commented that he had learned that she was going fishing out on the lake and that he had decided to come up to greet her and see if he and his team could get a free fish dinner.

He shook the Chief's hand and commented that it was good to see that the Chief of Detectives took such interest in his detectives that he went fishing with them. He asked if anyone had landed any fish before the excitement.

Alex asked if Harold had seen a black truck driving out. The answer was no.

She then asked for him to put out an APB on a black pickup with a matching black bed camper arrangement heading west.

Matt was sitting beside her and took her hand and wiped the blood off. He gave her a pill and some water to wash it down with. "For pain," was all he said.

Alex leaned in and put her head on his shoulder. She thanked him for the three-fifty-seven. She commented that Felix was not going to be happy about the condition of either of the boats he had rented.

When Felix came over and asked how she felt, he apologized about his school friend trying to kill her.

The fact that Felix knew the shooter immediately put new energy into her system.

She looked at Harold and asked if one of his integrators would interview Felix and see if there was anything that might be useful in tracking her shooter down.

She looked at the group now walking up the pier. She stood up and yelled if there was anyone who wanted to ride home in her car. She laughed when Nolan, Linda and Lorie ran up the pier toward her.

She had hoped for their reaction and wanted to get home and take what was becoming a daily routine to relax and relieve the tension in her body.

It was a relaxation that was similar to the calm before the storm.

She was going for the kill.

15 Escape from the Scene

Paul knew that the bounce of the boat had saved his life. She had a deadly aim. His zigzag and the bouncing boat had not kept him from getting hit three times. He now understood why Jeff and John were both dead. She had shot them holding the gun in her left hand. She was shooting at him with her right hand as he went by. He shook his head at the fact that she was a deadly shooter with either hand.

He had hoped the holes he had put into the bow below the water line would sink the yacht. But when he looked back he saw the yacht speeding after him. It was clear that whoever was at the helm knew what he was doing because the bow was up high above the water.

As he pulled away, Paul figured that he would easily beat the yacht back to the harbor but not by much.

Then the engine took a hit. He was amazed that she had been able to shoot and hit the engine. He thought he was beyond the range of her service pistol, but she must have had a bigger gun.

He saw that he was taking on water. She must also have put a hole in the hull.

He put the throttle all the way forward and hoped the engine would hold long enough for him to reach the harbor. He entered the harbor going as fast as the boat would go. He did not slow down but went full speed up the loading ramp and heard the engine rip out the transom. He was no longer concerned about the boat but was focused on getting to his truck.

He picked up his AR-15 and jumped up on the ramp walkway. A person was running toward him shouting about the way he had come in. He ran up toward the person and put down his shoulder and launched him into the water.

He did not stop but ran across the parking lot to his pickup. He threw the AR into the back took a moment to check on his wounds and then got behind the wheel and drove slowly out the road leading to the street.

He saw that the yacht had made the pier and watched as the person he had tried to kill jumped out and was racing toward the parking lot.

She had her pistol in hand as she raced full speed along the dock.

He sped up so that she would not have a shot. He now realized the deadly nature of his adversary.

He turned right as he got to the end of the harbor drive and in his rearview mirror saw a black van with the letters DEA driving in.

He hoped that they had not seen him.

He was now certain that he had misinterpreted the message he had assumed was for him that "the day would be his." His undoing he thought as he finished the thought.

He entered a small park and found a place to park that was not visible from the street. He wanted to use his first aid kit to patch himself up as best he could. It seemed that the bullet to his neck and his shoulder had both gone through and were clean. They had stopped bleeding. He could feel the bullet in his back but could not reach it to get it out. He hoped that it was close enough to the surface that any infection would push the bullet out. He hoped he could get to Mississippi and to the outfit that his two shooters had been a part of.

He knew he needed their help.

He figured his license plates would be on every highway patrol car screen. He looked around the park's parking lot and saw one pickup. He looked around and did not see anyone in the park. He figured that whoever owned the pickup had parked it and gotten a ride to work. He took off his license plates and put them on the red pickup and took the plates from the pickup and put it on his.

He planned to do this a couple of times more on his way south. He wished he could change the color of his truck but figured he did not have the time.

He headed west for several more hours and then turned south. He found a camper park and paid cash for a spot. After the sun set, he took off the plates on his pickup and took a walk.

He found a pickup that was parked in such a way that he could get to the front and back and not be seen by the folks that were in the camper.

He switched the plates and then headed back to his pickup and put on the plates.

At five the next morning he was on the road and figured he would make Mississippi and his goal by that evening. He drove slowly and remained below the speed limit. He had put out his two American flags on the two back doors.

He was hoping to send out the impression of a loyal American just taking his time driving south.

He found a park that was about three miles from the compound that his shooters had told him about. The wound in his back was oozing. He hoped that he could get it taken care of before it got any worse.

He walked through the woods and was unarmed.

He was stopped by three men armed with AR-15's who challenged him and threatened to shoot him.

Paul identified himself and mentioned the names of the two that had been sent to Cincinnati to help him take out the black female detective.

He was relieved when one of the three told him to follow and then turned and led the way through a gate that went through the tall fence with razor wire along the top.

He was impressed with the way the compound was fortified with the fence and then how the men were all armed with first class weapons.

He figured he would fit right in.

They then hiked for several miles through the woods. The other two followed behind him.

Once he they reached the main compound building, he was ushered into a large room where a silver haired old man sat at a table and told him to sit down and talk.

Paul sat down and then began by sharing the fact that he had been shot three times and had a bullet that was still in his back. He asked if that could be looked at before he recounted the story from the time of the shooting at the underpass in Cincinnati until now. He added that he had just come down from a confrontation with his intended target and knew that he had hit her.

He was relieved when the old man looked at one of the three that were standing behind him and told him to get Doc.

Paul hoped that Doc was a real doctor.

Doc came in and gave him a series of shots in the back to numb the area around the bullet wound. He then checked the two wounds that were to his arm and shoulder before addressing the one in his back.

When he turned his attention to the bullet in his back, he warned that even with the numbing there might still be quite a bit of pain.

Paul knew that he didn't have a choice and tried not to cry out as Doc took the bullet out of his back.

He instantly felt better and knew that he had come to the right place. He would be able to relax as he recovered from his wounds.

He then began sharing the tale from the time of the shooting under the bridge up to his arrival at the compound.

All he knew was that now he felt safe, and he would be able to relax during his recovery.

Little did he know that his recovery would be short-lived.

16 By the Pool

Alex gave each of the three a hug and led Nolan, Linda, and Lorie to her car. She waved back to Trey and Annie. She asked Matt to drive and got into her car. She had given her gun to Agent Zimmerman, but she had kept her holster. She readjusted her holster so that is was in front. She would put it away once she got back to the house.

Nolan asked her why they had been attacked. She thought for a moment and replied that there was a person that did not like her and was trying to kill her.

Linda and Lorie almost simultaneously comment that their father had tried to shoot her as well. They asked if he did not like her either.

Alex decided that she would not answer the question and deflected it by saying that it had been different, and they should ask their mother.

Once by the pool she asked Matt to watch the kids while she went up for a shower.

She encouraged the three to go swimming until lunch time. She told them she was sure they would have hamburgers or cheeseburgers as soon as all the food from the yacht was brought home.

When she came back to the pool, she let herself doze off. Her adrenalin had kept her going but she knew that she needed to let go and let her body relax.

She was not sure how long she had napped but her mother's voice directing people of where to put the food caused her to come awake.

The Chief and Harold came over and updated her on the crime scene investigation. Both the boat used by the shooter and the yacht were now out on dry dock. He said that the yacht would get fully repaired and the bullet holes would disappear.

Harold commented that the other boat would never see the water again and would be scrapped after it had been thoroughly examined. He was not certain whether the motor would be repairable.

They commented that Dexter, the owner of the marina and the boats could not stop apologizing for what had happened. He kept saying if he had known, he would never have rented the person who had been his old college friend a boat. He said that he would provide as many boats as needed to allow everyone that wanted to go fishing free of charge.

The Chief shared that the shooter had been hit several times and had lost a good amount of blood. Because the boat had flooded it was unclear how much the blood loss might have been. The blood sample was on its way to the lab to ascertain that it was that of Paul Grundle.

She was next approached by Bill and Trevor. They both thanked her for her quick action in getting everyone out of the line of fire. They had looked at the attack boat and complemented her on her shooting. They had counted four shots from her service revolver and that all seven shots from the three-fifty-seven had hit the back of the boat and the engine.

Trevor joked about making her the gun range master so she could teach all of them to shoot.

Johnnie and Mary came over.

Johnnie thanked her.

Mary simply said, "a black angel among us."

Johnnie asked if there was something he should be doing to help.

Alex asked him to dig into the two shooters from Mississippi. She wanted to know everything about who they associated with and why they would be willing to try to shoot a Cincinnati police detective.

Annie and Lindsey came over and thanked her for keeping them and their kids safe.

Lindsey touched Alex on her shoulder and commented that she had acted as a shield for her and Nolan.

She went on to say that Alex now had the same elevated lifelong status with her as Trey had expressed when he had been asked about how he felt about being saved by her.

Sandra walked over with two glasses of iced tea and gave a toast to her protector. She commented that she felt their roles seemed to be stuck in reverse. She shared that her bruises felt and looked awful.

She asked how Alex was feeling.

Ales quietly replied that she was miserable.

Alex watched as her father lit the grill and put on some hamburgers, hot dogs, and brats.

Her mother was putting out the buns, relishes, and fixings.

She dosed off again and awoke when she heard Felix's voice.

He had come over to see how she was feeling. He made the point that she had been one of his longest customers and he felt awful about her having been shot.

When he asked if there was anything that he could do, Alex told him she was not holding anything against him but if he brought her a Cheeseburger he would earn a gold star.

Not long after Linda and Lori came over and said that they wanted to be just like her.

Alex looked at them and said that she wished she could be just like their mother and that their mother created art that made people see the world with a beauty that brought them happiness.

She said that they should learn from her and try to be as skilled as she was.

The two of left and ran to their mother and gave her a hug and said they wanted to create beauty like she did.

Matt looked at her and commented that he was impressed with how she had deflected the two girls admiration for her to their mother.

Alex nodded and replied that everything she had said was true. She wished her talent with her gun could be leveraged to something that created beauty.

Mary-Anne who had been sitting nearby commented that the Chief thought that Alex was creating beauty by taking out the ugly elements of society.

She was surprised when Trey added that he hoped that she would continue to act as she normally did and track down every offender she chose to pursue.

He planned to always have her back.

The comments lifted her mentally but between the bruises on her chest and back and fresh bullet wound to her right shoulder she was beginning to feel miserable.

It was still early but she was ready to go sleep.

She walked over and sat down near her father and let him know that she did not feel like getting up early to go fishing but that she wanted him to get the group out and fishing. She would wait for the late lunch feast when the group returned.

She made the rounds and wished everyone luck on the fishing trip the following morning and let them know that she was not going.

She then went up to her room and again stood under the shower. The wound on her shoulder was sealed to be watertight and withstood the long shower.

She came out to find Matt sitting on the easy chair. He had come up to check on her.

She gave him a hug and told him that she just needed rest. She showed him her bruises that were beginning to show.

He touched one and asked if it hurt and that it looked terrible.

Alex gave a small laugh and said that it seemed that every part of her body hurt. She said that she hoped an idle day just sitting or lying by the pool would help.

Matt let her know that he would come back later and hoped he would not wake her.

Alex told him not to worry about waking her and that she planned to be out until morning.

<u>17 Mississippi Sheriff</u>

James knew immediately who was calling. He had given his best friend the rattle of machine gun fire for a ring tone. The two were best friends and had shared combat in Iraq and Afghanistan.

He said hello and asked why it had taken him so long to call. He said the Ohio Highway Patrol had contacted him and asked about two Mississippi residents that had IDs that gave Wiggins as their addresses.

He learned from them that three people had been targeted. They named you, Alex and a third person that was a new name but who had been assigned to guard Alex. That sounded a lot like the last person that guarded Alex.

I had to marry her to save her.

"Did you call to update me, or do you need my help," he finished.

He listened as Matt filled him in on the details from the time of the attack on Alex when she was going to work. Then he described the second attack that ended up under the interstate highway overpass.

He finished with the attack that had just happened out on Lake Michigan where the entire department had come to go fishing.

Matt explained that this last attack had endangered the entire department and their families, and that Alex was angrier then he had ever seen her.

She was planning to come down and personally interrogate the group that called themselves, "Patriots for A better Future."

She was sure that they had conspired with the person, Paul Grundle, to set up the second shooting.

She had killed the two while being hit more than four times. Her bodyguard had been hit three times.

They had all survived because Alex had insisted they all wear the Kevlar vests.

James let out a long breath and replied that he would look into the group again.

Nothing about the two that had been killed in Cincinnati had caused anyone locally to put in a missing person's report.

He had a call into Chief Johnson but had not received a call back.

He would be more than happy to facilitate questioning the group.

He stated that a warrant would be needed to even get on to the property to do so.

He would put in the paperwork and get a warrant ready.

That evening he shared the details with Abbie.

She looked at him and responded that had she returned to continue working with Alex, she would have been that person doing the guarding.

She went on to say that Alex's guards usually were too slow to do any guarding.

She pointed out that Alex was called "Cincinnati's Black Annie Oakley" for a reason.

The people attacking her normally were the ones to die.

James agreed with her and gave her a hug. He said that he was lucky that Alex had brought her into his life and that she had stayed.

He got the folks in his department finding out all they could about the Patriots.

The more he learned about them the less patriotic the organization came out to be. They were more anti-government than patriotic.

It was hard to find out about the individuals that were members.

James recruited several of his deputies to make the rounds of the bars and restaurants and see what they could find out about the Patriots.

The picture that slowly emerged was not the one that anyone expected.

James was surprised to learn that one member was a bartender at a popular pub often frequented by his team. One was a member on the city council. And the third one identified was a clerk at the local hardware store.

James decided that he should check out the addresses that had been sent to him by the Ohio Highway Patrol. He had two names; a Samuel Remington and the other was Henry Williams.

He looked up the names in the county registry. He found the address for a Henry and Wilma Williams. There was a Remington family registered but he could not find a specific address for Samuel.

He decided to check out the address for Williams.

When he arrived at the address, he saw that a tan sedan was parked in the driveway.

He parked behind the sedan, walked to the front door, and rang the bell.

A plain looking, woman answered the door and asked what he wanted.

He asked if he might come in and ask a few questions.

He was surprised when she asked if she had to let him in.

He replied that she did not.

She asked again what he wanted.

He asked if she had heard from her husband.

Her reply was, "What business is that to you?"

He then said that the Ohio State Police had informed him that a person of that name had been shot and killed in Cincinnati.

He watched as the person in front of him crumbled and fell to her knees.

James held out his hand and helped her up.

He asked if he could take her in and get her a glass of water. The house he walked into was neat and clean.

It was clear to him that the woman was a good housekeeper.

He walked down the hallway toward what he thought was the kitchen. On the way he passed a room that had a gun rack that had a large assortment of rifles.

There was one empty rack.

He returned to the living room with the glass of water.

He asked her name and got the response he expected, "Wilma"

He let Wilma know that he would be getting a judge to give him the authority to search her house.

He was pleased by her response that he could search any time he wanted.

He thanked her and went out to his car and called for backup units so two people would search the house.

He knew that he had found one of the shooters and the empty gun rack that would hold the weapon that was currently in Cincinnati.

He asked Wilma if she knew a Samuel Remington.

He saw her react and say that he was one of her husband's drinking buddies.

He instructed the two officers that had arrived. He let them know that he was going to the next address to determine if it was the residence where Samuel Remington lived.

His greeting at the Remington home was the opposite of his reception at the Williams' home. The couple that stood at the door commented that they had both voted for him.

He thanked them and asked if they had a moment for him to talk with them.

He was escorted into a sitting area and offered something to drink. He thanked them but thought it would be better for them to talk first.

When asked about where Samuel might be. They looked at each other and asked what crazy thing that had he might have done.

James took a deep breath and said that he thought that Samuel had been shot and killed along with Henry Williams.

The two had gone to Cincinnati with the intension of shooting and killing a Cincinnati Police detective.

The couple silently hugged each other and then asked if the body would be returned to Wiggins.

James assured them that the bodies would be coming back to Wiggins but that they would be held in Cincinnati until the coroner released them for transport.

They both continued to hug each other.

He gave them his condolence, let them know that he would contact them when it was time to claim the body and left to return to the office.

Once there he contacted Matt as well as Chief Johnson.

18 On the Trail

In her dreams Alex was trying to fire her weapon.

The killer was getting away.

She was running as fast as she could but every time she looked she was in the same place. She sat bolt upright and realized that she was having a nightmare.

She looked out her window and saw that it was daylight. She wondered what time in the morning it might be.

Matt's side of the bed let her know that he had joined her last night and had left to go fishing.

She looked over to where the large green numbers on the clock flicked and clearly let her know that it was nine in the morning.

This was a new record for her. She had not slept this long since her college days and she recalled that those long sleeps were most often after drinking too much.

She had regained control of her life by joining AA and following their guidance. She learned to control her drinking.

She had no idea how to control not getting shot at and there was no guidance for that.

She decided that a hot cup of tea, some toast and maybe a bowl of yogurt would help. After getting dressed in a pair of shorts and a yellow T-shirt she took the backstairs to the kitchen.

She was surprised to see her Mother, Mary, Mary-Anne, and Sandra all sitting at the table. Her mother asked what she wanted for breakfast.

Sandra said that she had stayed behind to assume her protection duties.

Mary and Mary-Anne added that they did not feel like fishing.

Alex poured herself a cup of coffee and sat down. She asked if there were any news from those out fishing.

Her mother told her that when her father arrived at the harbor he was met by Felix who pointed at the yacht and said that it was all patched up and fit to take them all out fishing. The yacht had been outfitted with poles, bait and there was a breakfast box for everyone. Felix insisted that he would take the boat out and make sure everyone had a memorable time. He said he could not ensure everyone would catch a fish, but he wanted everyone to relax and have a good time.

Alex had just finished her yogurt when she got a call from Matt. He let her know that the fishing was great. He thought that everyone had already caught at least one fish.

He said he was calling because James's investigation had resulted in linking the two shooters that had attacked them at the overpass to an organization called the "Patriots for a better Future." James was standing by before taking any action by himself.

He was getting all the legal paperwork to speed up getting the guilty parties extradited to Ohio.

The Chief called not long after Matt had hung up. He let her know that he had talked with Sheriff Kaizer and that he would be sending her and Trey down to Wiggins the following week. He said that officer Olson would also be going with her with the duty as her guard.

Alex replied that she was looking forward to the trip. She then asked him how the fishing was going and learned that he had caught two large bass and that it seemed everyone was getting their fish. He was sure that the three kids had caught several fish based on all the yelling and cheering coming from their location.

He said that her father wanted to talk with her.

Her dad made the point that he missed her but said that everyone was having a great time. He had fired up the grill and was getting ready to serve hot dogs, burgers, and brats. He hoped she would have a restful day and said that later she and he would have to catch up.

After hanging up, Alex looked around at the women at the table and asked if they regretted not going fishing. They all laughed and said that sitting at the table and being able to relax and chat was much more of an attractive exercise.

Alex nodded in agreement but even as she did she was texting Johnnie that his next miracle assignment was to learn all he could about the organization, "Patriots for a Better Future."

She moved from the kitchen table to a reclining lounge chair on the shaded side of the pool.

Sandra positioned her chair so that she was in the sun. She took off her shorts and tank top. She had her bikini on underneath. She put on suntan lotion and then lay back with her tear drop sunglasses over her eyes.

Alex commented that her purple bruises complemented her white skin. She then said that she was feeling a little vulnerable and asked her where her protection weapon might be and got the reply that it was under her bikini but Sandra pointed her finger to the bag on the floor by her side.

Alex and Sandra were still out by the pool when her mother asked if they were interested in lunch.

Alex said she would wait until the early afternoon meal when the fishing crew returned.

Sandra simply said, "ditto." She had moved her chair next to Alex's and they were both sipping on a glass of iced tea.

When Alex let Sandra know that she would be going to Wiggins, Mississippi, she was asked by Sandra about the last time that she had been in Wiggins.

Sandra said she had heard all sort of stories about what had happened in Wiggins and how she got the name "Cincinnati's Black Annie Oakley" while she was there.

Alex chuckled at the question. She said that Matt was to blame for that handle, but she had forgiven him and had chosen instead to fall in love with him.

She was reciting what had happened when she said she had to stop so that she could make some notes about what she wanted Johnnie to research.

She said that she called him the miracle man because for every case he had provided the critical information that had led her to a breakthrough. It had just come to her what she needed him to do. She texted him a note with her request.

Mary had quietly been sitting in a lounge chair not far away.

She shared that Johnnie had just sent her a message that he wanted to have his computer out by the pool. He said he had gotten his marching orders from his boss to get on the trail. He had his computer with him but he was not having muck luck connecting while he was on the Golden Goose. He wanted to jump right on it, but he wanted to do it sipping on a cool one out by the pool.

Alex gave a little laugh and said that she seldom got called boss but that she would be glad to help get everything set up the way Johnnie wanted it.

As she stood up she realized how bad she felt.

Her whole body ached.

The wound in her right shoulder was also letting her know that she needed to take it easy.

She decided that one of the things she needed to take was her over the counter pain pill.

She asked Sandra if she wanted a pain pill and a refill of her iced tea.

She had just finished asking when her mother carried out a tray with two new glasses of iced tea at the serving window and two pills on a plate.

Alex gave her mother a hug and took one of the glasses and one pill. She sat down and after swallowing her pill leaned back in the lounge chair and closed her eyes.

This case, she thought, was different in that it seemed to keep taking energy out of her.

She knew that somehow she had to step up and take control.

She would soon learn that even at her low energy state she would have ten times the stamina of those around her.

She just did not realize the power of the adrenaline she generated when she was threatened.

19 Partner

Trey was having a great time. Nolan and he had fished together and had both caught two very nice fish. Lindsey wasn't fishing but she handled the net with which to bring the fish on board and then had helped carry them to the holding tank at the back of the yacht.

It was great to listen to Nolan when he was reeling in his catch.

Trey noticed that Lindsey was quiet, and he knew that she had been shocked by the action on the day before and was still processing what had happened.

He knew her reaction was similar to a recruit after their first time in combat.

Once they were safely back in camp they would often seem dazed and disoriented.

When Nolan was fishing, Trey would put his arms around Lindsey and the two of them would silently watch Nolan.

He whispered to her that she should skateboard the Mall of America and remember the surge of exhilaration she felt when doing so and that it would help.

He knew that Bill and Trevor were helping the two girls with their fishing. They were helping the two with netting the fish they caught. Annie was also fishing and the commotion they were raising had caused Nolan to ask if he could fish over where his two friends were.

Trey got Bill and Trevor to change sides and he, Linsey and Nolan moved to the side Annie and her two were fishing.

He had stopped fishing and was just enjoying helping with the kids.

The Chief had shared the news from Wiggins and said that if Alex was up to it they should head south and see if the case could be closed.

Trey shared this news with Lindsey who commented that Alex would jump at the chance whether she felt good or not. She made the point that he should step up and do most of the driving.

She then stopped and asked if the two of them would have a car.

Lindsey laughed when he replied that the Chief had assured him that the oldest car on the lot was being processed, cleaned, and made ready for recycling by the Evercrest demolition team. The car would have a bullet proof wind shield and the best engine possible and one that would keep running even after being hit repeatedly by machine gun fire.

Linsey gave him a hug and quietly said that she wanted him to be super careful. She thanked him for reminding her of the Mall of America.

It had helped and she felt much better.

The Chief had been watching Trey, Bill, and Trevor. It was clear that his two best investigative teams had bonded.

Hiring Alex had made a significant difference. She had not only solved numerous tough cases, but she had also had a significant impact on him and on the entire police department.

Several of the very biased police personnel had chosen to quit the force but the majority were now proud at the successes and the recognition that Alex had brought to the Cincinnati Police Department.

The Police Chief, his boss, seemed to have changed his stripes as well.

And issuing a new car to Alex now had no barriers.

This was especially true since Alex had suggested that she get the oldest car in the department assigned to her.

He had agreed because he did not think that he could push another request for a new car through the approval process. He was able to make sure that whatever car she drove would be in top shape and give her as much protection as possible.

He stopped his contemplation as he was almost pulled overboard by whatever had hit his line. He was surprised at how long he had to fight what was on his line. He was wearing out as he slowly played the fish and brought it toward the boat. He was exhausted and happy that Alex's father had the net ready to help him.

Together the two of them managed to get a huge Pike up on the deck. He knew immediately that he was going to get this one mounted and hung up on the wall in his office.

Everyone came over to look at the fish he had hauled in.

He sat down and accepted a beer and said that he was done fishing.

Trey came over and congratulated the Chief on his catch. The three kids were looking at the fish as it was lowered into the holding area. Bill and Trevor came over and Trevor commented that he now understood why he was called the Chief.

Johnnie came over and after congratulating him on his catch, let the Chief know that his boss had given him his marching orders. He was to report for duty by the pool back at the house and do research, but he really needed to start with a beer before working on his vacation.

Trey hugged Lindsey who was now sitting on the edge of his chair. He knew that he had found the city and the department where he wanted to work. He also knew that his work partner was the one responsible for how everyone on board had found new meaning to their lives.

He thought about the fact that she was petite, very good looking, a runner, a biker but most of all she made sure those around her were focused on improving and treating each other with respect.

He raised his beer and said, "to Alex" and was pleased to see that everyone responded with, "to Alex."

Felix came over to the Chief and asked if he wanted the Pike mounted. He said he would arrange for getting it mounted and later shipped to Cincinnati.

Trey saw a smile cross the Chief's face as he said that he indeed wanted it mounted. He said that he wanted a brass plaque to be on the mounting board that said "The Evercrest Pike. The biggest fish I ever caught" and he gave a date that caught Trey by surprise. He knew that it was the date that Alex had been hired.

Trey smiled and proposed a toast to the Evercrest Pike.

It was apparent that the fishing was over. Felix said he would take the yacht in slowly and that everyone should relax and enjoy the early afternoon.

Trey accepted another brat from Alex's father who was trying to clear all the grilled meats that had been prepared. It had been a great morning. He saw that Nolan had fallen asleep in his chair. Everyone was now sitting and enjoying the ride back in.

He commented that it was one of the best fishing trips that he had been on. He pointed out that it was not as exciting as the one the day before but one that they all deserved.

Trey raised his glass when Matt made a toast to Alex's dad and the great grill master that he was.

Trey asked Matt how Alex was doing.

He listened as Matt shared that Alex was disappointed that her attacker had escaped. She planned to get on the offensive and take the action to him.

He said that he was a little worried that she was pushing herself too much but added that she was recovering well from all her bruises she had.

Little did he know the intensity and the challenge of the offensive action that Alex would unleash.

20 A "New" Car

The Thursday dinner was a huge success. Everyone praised the Chief for catching the biggest fish. Everyone had caught a fish, and most were taking their fish home on dry ice. The talk was about how much excitement they had on the first day and the fun they had on the second day.

Alex enjoyed the evening but was happy that she would have a few days at home with just Matt, her parents and Sandra. Their flight back to Cincinnati was on Sunday afternoon.

The next day she chose to sit by the pool and relax. It was clear to her that her body had taken a huge hit and just wanted to rest. She figured the coming week would have her focused on tracking and apprehending Paul Grundle.

She kept repeating to herself that she would give him every opportunity to give himself up, but she knew she would not hesitate to shoot him.

She got to know Sandra better than she had expected. Sandra told her that she had started to date the police officer that had been assigned the second shift guard duty.

Alex asked when she had time for a date and laughed when Sandra explained that the dates had been picnics in the hallway outside of her apartment.

Sandy smiled and said that her mother had always told her to leverage any opportunity that presented itself. And said that a certain person who she was assigned to protect had her so busy that the only opportunity was to think of the hallway as a park. She said that the tenant across the hall from Alex's had come out and given them a slice of apple pie and ice cream on one occasion.

Alex offered to get someone else to be her guard if Sandra wanted a chance at some real dates.

Sandra countered that she would never have met her current date if it were not for the assignment to guard her. She said that it might not be as exciting as what happened to the last woman to have been assigned to guard her, but she hoped it would have a similar outcome.

Alex nodded and thought about her situation and the realization she was the victim of a hate crime.

She knew she was experiencing the psychological stress associated with this kind of crime.

There was no action that she had taken and other than the color of her skin there was no reason for the attack.

She was used to being attacked by the criminal that was being pursued. They were openly the bad guys, and she had no problem dealing with their actions.

But dealing with someone that could hate so much that he would attack her for being black or of a different persuasion was something that was hard for her to process.

It just did not fit any of the categories that she placed people in.

Then it hit her that she had not really understood Black history as well as she should have. She decided to study it with an eye to all the hate that she was now sensitized to.

She had talked this out with Matt and together they had decided they would do two strategic things.

First was to contact the department psychologist so they could talk through being made the victim because of her skin color and the impact that it had on her.

The second was to take several courses focused on the American Black experience offered at the university.

She had been surprised at how quickly she had gotten an appointment with the apartment psychologist. It seemed to her that she had been expected.

They were both surprised that they had more trouble enrolling in the university class because they were not registered as students.

She, Matt, and Sandy spent the rest of the weekend walking the beach in the early morning and spending the rest of the day by the pool either relaxing or on their computers.

Her parents made sure that they all had some great meals together but otherwise stayed in the background.

Back in Cincinnati on Monday morning Alex decided to ride her bike on the same route that she had used on the day she was attacked.

Figuratively it was like getting back on your horse after getting bucked off. She rode past the library where a shiver went down her back but otherwise the ride into work was anticlimactic. Sandy had arranged for a bike and followed behind her.

When she got to the office, she got herself a cup of coffee and sat down at her desk.

Sandy took a chair to the side.

Officially Alex had the whole week off, but she had arranged to meet with the department psychologist first thing.

She wanted to think through what she might say. It was not clear to her how the session would go.

Trey walked in and had a surprised look on his face. He asked her what she was doing at her desk and that he had heard the Chief say she had the week off.

Alex replied that she had come to work to get her half of the bear claw they always shared and that afterward she would go home.

Trey smiled and said that she would have to wait until Bill and Trevor brought in the morning donuts and sweets.

Alex then let him know that she had an appointment to talk with the psychologist and that she had heard that a trip to Mississippi was in the works.

She said she did not want the Chief to assign that trip to anyone but the three of them.

The Chief walked over where the three were sitting and bade them good morning and said that he saw that his suggestion of taking the week off had been ignored.

Alex gave him her cover reason for being there.

The Chief smiled and said that he approved of her seeking some counseling.

He then asked them to step into his office.

Alex was expecting a lecture but was pleasantly surprised that the chief instead put a holster and a revolver on his desk and said that he would issue it to her when she returned with a clearance from her counselor and a certification from the firing range master.

The Chief went on to say that her "new" car was ready and that he had been assured it would make a trip to Mississippi and back with no problem. He had been told that the engine was one of the bigger ones and was in good enough shape that it would make 120 mph plus. He said that he was not suggesting that she drive any faster than the speed limit but pointing out that the car was in top shape and other than its age was the best running one.

Alex thanked him for the "new" car and told him that she would keep it in one piece for as long as she could but so far she had been safe but somehow her luck and the luck of her cars was dismally low.

Alex left the office.

Matt waked in wearing his uniform and together they went to meet with the psychologist.

She had met with Dr. Allengardner before, but those meetings had been debriefings about how she had felt after shooting and killing a bad guy.

At those meetings she had shared that she was always surprised at how her attackers had been given the chance to surrender and had always chosen to ignore that offer.

Dr. Allengardner greeted both of them and asked if having Matt present would cause Alex any hesitations with what she wanted to discuss.

Alex shook her head and said that he was a key supporter and had been present in the last several attacks.

Dr. Allengardner said that she would have preferred to wait another week and a few more sessions before clearing her to be armed but she had learned from the Chief of Detectives that he needed her to go to Mississippi and he wanted her to have a weapon.

Alex thanked her and agreed to weekly sessions for the next few weeks.

Alex then shared that in the last five encounters she had immediately chosen to shoot when she had been ignored. She worried that perhaps she was being too aggressive

The session went longer than expected but she walked out feeling relieved. She asked Matt how he felt about the session.

He said that he felt better about how the two of them should handle their feelings. He said that together they would both work back to the position of feeling confident in their actions.

She made the point that this first session had lifted a big weight off her shoulders.

She went directly from the counseling to the firing range where she easily qualified.

Sandra asked if Alex would give her some tips on improving her skills on the range.

Alex said that the range master would train her on the basics of holding her weapon and how to breath. She should listen and follow his instructions until it was as if she were breathing.

Then all she had to do was to practice, practice and when she thought she was improving she should practice some more.

She walked back to the Chief's office where the Chief simply commented that it had taken her longer than he had expected.

The Chief had Sandra, Trey, Bill, and Trevor all bear witness to his official reinstatement of Alex to be armed.

He had a separate official looking piece of paper labeled the "Evercrest Automobile Promise" that declared that Alex would do her best not to get her newly assigned car blown up, shot up or burnt to a cinder.

He made her sign and had the rest put their witnessing signature on it as well.

Alex burst out laughing when the Chief led the way to the main entrance area bulletin board and put it up.

She commented that it was not fair to put the blame on her when every car had been done in by one of the criminals that she eventually nailed.

They left the bulletin board as a group of people gathered around it to see what had been posted. She could hear the laughter all the way back her desk.

It was music to her ears.

<u>21 Arrival to Wiggins</u>

*T*rey had insisted that he drive.

Sandra had volunteered that she was also willing to drive.

Alex said that she was pleased to have two skilled drivers that were eager to do the driving. She said she would sit in the passenger side and enjoy the view.

She was relieved that she would be able to relax and let her body recover from all the bruises and from the wound on her right shoulder.

A few minutes later, she looked back to where Sandra was sitting behind Trey and dozing.

She knew that Sandra had pushed herself to stay on duty and had admitted to Alex that she felt like death warmed over and confessed that she was not as tough as she saw her able to be.

Alex knew Trey would most likely do most if not all of the driving.

She was anxious to get to Wiggins. She was certain that Paul Grundle was somewhere in the vicinity. She had tracked the reports of stolen pickup license plates.

The ones she had been interested in came from Rockford, Illinois and then Des Moines Iowa, the final report came from St. Louis, Missouri. She figured that Paul had gone west for a period of time and then turned south. She figured that from St. Louis he would have gone straight south to Wiggins. She looked at the map and tried to figure out where in the Wiggins area he might have sought refuge.

She contacted Johnnie to see if he had found the location of the group, Patriots for a better America." Johnnie replied that he had found the location of the property where the compound was located.

He had also been able to identify several of the members of the group. One member of the group was an employee of the main local hardware store.

Another was the mayor of Wiggins.

A third was the principle of the high school.

They all had their names on the deed for the property where the compound was located.

He said there were other names, but he did not know where they were located, and he would continue to work on that.

Alex had her phone on speaker phone so that Trey could hear.

Sandra spoke up and commented to Johnnie that she now understood why Alex called him her miracle worker.

Alex asked Johnnie to update the Chief and then make sure that Sheriff Kaizer was brought up to date.

She hung up and placed a call to Matt and told him to call the Sheriff and let him know that she would appreciate having him investigate the involvement of Wiggin's Mayor and the Principle of the High School with the Patriots for America group.

The lunch stop gave Alex a chance to do some stretching. It let her know that her body was barely back to normal.

Sandra commented that it was too painful for her to touch her toes and could not believe Alex could do all the exercises that she was doing.

Alex sat down at the table outside of the fast food restaurant. She had ordered a double layer cheeseburger with all the trimmings.

She noted that Trey was not eating lunch. She asked if he was alright.

Trey responded that he was saving himself for a steak dinner.

She knew that he had told her he did not eat if he was driving because it made him sleepy.

She offered to do some of the driving, but he declined.

It was around six in the evening when Alex next awoke.

Sandra commented that Alex had been out since around one.

Alex learned they were about two thirds of the way to Wiggins. She followed Trey into the hotel lobby.

She noticed that there was a Steak Restaurant next door. The number of cars in their lot indicated that it was popular.

They were all on the departments expense, but she jokingly said she would buy Trey his steak as soon as they were checked in.

Later after a great steak and a glass of a smooth non-alcoholic red wine, Alex stood under a hot shower and absorbed the heat.

She knew that her body was slowly getting back to its normal condition.

She was getting ready to climb into bed when a weird feeling came over her.

She went to the front door to her room and wedged a chair under the door handle.

She then did the same to the bedroom door.

The lights from the helicopter gunship brightly illuminated the room. Alex jumped up and ran out of the room as the two rotating machine guns began ripping through the room. It took out the center wall and did the same with the front wall of the room. Alex ran down the hall and descended two flights to Johnnie's room. Johnnie asked her what was wrong. Alex told him to get his clothes and follow her. She led the way down and to the side door. Once outside she located the Helicopter. It had landed in the parking lot and only the pilot was still with the craft. She had Johnnie run a cable through the landing legs and hook it to a hydrant. The thugs that had been in to check that she was dead climbed back into the helicopter.

She walked out to get the helicopter to come after her. It was then she realize she was still totally naked and they were all pointing at her and laughing.

She woke up and realized that she was dreaming about what had happened in her last case. She had not been naked in that situation, but she had caused the helicopter to crash and burn.

Alex was totally soaked and decided that a morning shower was in order.

She again stood under the hot shower. She realized that this case was having a greater effect on her than all the other cases combined.

Being violently attacked just for being black had an effect that she had not anticipated.

She stood for a long time under the shower and thought through many of her cases and knew that she was going to solve this case as she had done all the rest.

She went down and after breakfast they all got in the car and continued the drive to Wiggins.

She dosed on and off as Trey continued to drive to Wiggins.

Early in the afternoon she was happy to see the hotel in Wiggins where they would stay. She was looking forward to an early dinner meeting with Sheriff Kaiser and Abbie.

She took the time to connect with Johnnie to see if he had anything else to share.

Johnnie had continued to scour the internet to see what he could find on the Patriots for a better America. He had found some additional pictures of various members at a rally, but he had not been able to put names to them but was working on that.

He said that he had a better view of the compound that he was sending her. The map or layout was to scale. She would be able to figure out the exact distances associated with the layout.

He said that he was working to see if he could find the drawings for the buildings in the compound but said that they probably did not exist in a public computer system.

Alex took a quick look at the compound and then went to dinner. She planned to come back and study it in detail before going to bed.

The multiple passes of studying the details and then envisioning how to enter the compound would later serve to save the lives of all of the team.

It was great to see Abbie. She introduced Sandra to her and said that she was having a hard time keeping her alive but she had been successful in getting her to have a fiancé that was in law enforcement. She suggested that the two of them compare notes on how to manage such a situation.

She then focused her attention on the Sheriff. She listened as he shared that fact that he had all the paperwork that would make extradition to Ohio and to arrest all those associated with the group.

He suggested that they have breakfast and get into the details of how to apprehend the group. He made the point that they needed to have the proper evidence to make sure they could make the arrests stick.

22 Compound Perimeter

Over breakfast Alex, Trey and Sandra looked over the map of the compound and discussed it with Sheriff Kaizer.

She planned to walk around the perimeter of the compound to get a feel for its layout and size. She also wanted to see its fencing.

The one overhead shot showing a section of the fence showed what looked like a ten foot chain link fence.

Sheriff Kaizer said he only knew of one gate where the property came to the public road. He commented that it would be a gate that would be very difficult to get through. He was not sure if the department had a vehicle that would go through the locked gate.

Alex asked whether anyone had a snowplow truck.

That brought a laugh from the Sheriff, and he said that yes he would show her the dozen that they needed to clear the snow from the highways around the Wiggins during the raging winters.

Then he smiled and said that he had a friend that worked a lumber company that had several very large log loaders that could easily run through the gate. He would arrange to have one close by when Alex made her way into the compound.

Alex said that her team needed to stay closely coordinated with the Wiggins team and would keep him informed.

The Sheriff asked if she expected a confrontation. Alex responded that two of the group's members had traveled to Cincinnati to shoot her.

She figured they might be just as trigger happy on their home turf.

The Sheriff pointed out the best place to leave her car. He made a point that the approach to the compound would be through the forest. They should be able to remain undetected during the tour of the perimeter.

He agreed with Alex that he and his team should standby incase shooting started but that there was not good reason for them to be with Alex and her team. His team would be ready to rush in and provide support.

He made the point that the Mayor of Wiggins was listed on the property deed as one of the owners. He was ready for any moves by the Mayor and if the group was brought to trial he would make sure the Mayor would be part of the group. He said that he had already quietly processed the paperwork to remove the Mayor from office.

Alex drove to the location where she would leave the car. She opened the trunk and made sure everyone donned their bullet proof vests. Sandra commented that she hoped she would not have to turn in her new vest with flattened bullets embedded in it as she had done just two weeks ago.

Alex made the point that she would walk out in front. She had Trey and Sandra each take a spot that was at least ten feet behind her and maintain the same space between them. They would be staggered so if there was an encounter they would not be in each other's line of fire.

Trey commented that he was impressed that both Sandra and Alex had gotten hit and then had gone to Alex's home and gone fishing and were now getting ready to walk several miles through the woods.

Alex smiled and responded that women were tougher than they looked.

She then made sure each of them had extra rounds for their weapons.

She then said to follow her and led the way through the woods.

Alex saw the fence ahead and signaled for a right turn. She looked back to make sure Trey and Sandra were in position.

Trey was dressed in a green and brown checkered shirt, tan Dockers, and hiking boots.

Sandra had a long sleeve blouse similar to Trey's shirt, dark green pants, and hiking boots.

She figured that her black blouse, black Dockers, and black boots made her the least woodsy looking, but it matched her mood.

She was carefully looking into the compound so that she could both understand its layout and also not be surprised by anyone on the other side.

She had moved slowly along the perimeter for about twenty minutes when motion out ahead of her made her stop. She knelt down and made sure Trey and Sandra had followed suit and were in position.

The movement she had spotted was of three men in what looked like full tactical gear with what she took to be AR-15's out in front of her on her side of the fence. She looked along the fence and spotted a gate that remained open.

She looked up in the trees that bordered the fence and thought she spotted a small camera unit. She figured the three of them had been spotted.

She slowly drew her weapon and took off the safety.

She called out to the three ahead of her. They had not yet located her but turned in the direction of her voice. She heard the clicks of safeties being disengaged.

When the person closest to her began to fire his weapon, she shot him in the inside of his left foot. He began to fall but as he did his firing AR-15 hit his two buddies in the chest. He began to bring the gun back around to where Alex was kneeling when her second shot hit him in the jaw just behind his face shield.

She knew it was a kill shot.

Trey followed Alex's example and took out the second shooter. Sandra emptied her revolver into the third shooter but did little more that make him stagger back. As he brought his weapon around, Alex shot him in the side of his foot and then as he fell the exposed jaw area.

She moved quickly forward and made sure the shooters were dead.

She moved the AR-15's away from the bodies and into the woods.

She then reloaded her weapon and put it back into her holster.

She complemented Trey and Sandra for doing their part.

She called the Sheriff and explained the situation. He agreed to send a team in to the location where the fight had occurred, and he was also sending a car to the compound entrance.

She let him know the approximate location and told him she was leaving her phone as a marker for him to locate the exact spot.

Alex took her phone and placed it on the ground next to one of the shooters.

She then led the way into the compound. She was now determined to get to the compound and to apprehend anyone there.

Her heightened senses were about to save the three of them again and she would continue to handout final departure tickets to hell to anyone shooting at her.

<u>*23 Compound Proper*</u>

Alex knew that the only way in was through the open gate and the camera high in the tree was aimed straight toward the gate. She put her arm down on a low tree limb and aimed just above the camera lens and took a shot.

She took it out on the second shot. She quickly reloaded her weapon.

She knew that the folks that monitored the camera knew that they were going to have intruders entering. She jogged toward the gate with her weapon drawn.

She now had probable cause and planned to make a B-line to the main compound area.

The map of the area was clear in her mind, and she wanted to get to the compound building as quickly as possible.

She had Sandra and Trey close the gap between them. She looked back and saw a red spot on Sandra. She launched herself at Sandra and felt the bullet hit her in the back.

Trey immediately opened fire toward the top of the ridge to their left.

Alex recovered and put three shots into the same area and saw an AR-15 slide down the hill. She immediately ran toward the hill side looking for additional shooters. A trail of bullets followed her. She used the last of her bullets to respond and heard a curse and then she saw one of the attackers running up and then disappearing as he went over the top.

She reloaded as she ran up the hill and went over to where she found two dead shooters. She threw their weapons down to Trey and observed that Sandra had her weapon out and was slowly turning to make sure there were no other shooters.

She put in a call to the sheriff and let him know about the additional dead attackers and that she was continuing toward the main compound.

After making sure everyone was Ok, she took up a jog toward the compound. She was moving as fast as she dared and was using all the cover she could.

They took fire as they got to the compound perimeter. Alex took up a position behind a panel truck. Sandra suddenly shouted that two shooters were behind them.

The lead person was raising a shotgun as Alex turned. As she shot, she recognized him as Paul Grundle the person she was seeking. Her shots were reflexive, and Paul was dead before he could raise the barrel and pull the trigger.

The second person was raising an AR-15 as Trey shot and killed him with the same three shot pattern used by Alex.

Several shots came from the barn. Alex decided to utilize the AK-15 laying by the body of the second attacker. She ran out from behind the truck and took cover behind the body as another round of bullets hit. She made sure the safety was off on the AR and then rolled out into the open and strategically shot bullets at the person hiding behind the pickup in front of the barn. She put two bullets on either side of the front tire and was rewarded by the person behind it falling to the ground as he screamed in pain. She put a zigzag series of shots across the two large sliding barn doors. The cursing indicated successful hits. Each time she shot she rolled on the ground to a new position.

She stood up and rushed toward the front door of the main building while taking periodic shots at the barn door. She watched Trey roll out and take two shots at the person on the ground behind the truck.

She entered the compound's main building and announced that she was the police. She heard a person in the next room say they gave up and not to shoot.

She entered the room that looked like a central control room for a flight tower. There were at least a dozen mounted screens that had various scenes around the compound. Her eyes caught the scene out in front of the barn and the area that she had just been in.

She witnessed the arrival of the Sheriff and four of his deputies.

She instructed her captive to come out from under the table and walk outside with his hands over his head.

She loudly announced her intension to come out and had the person in front of her to walk out.

She put the AR and the weapon she had confiscated down inside of the building and walked out with her hands in the air.

The Sheriff thanked her and told her to put her hands down.

She walked over to where Trey and Sandra were standing and gave them a group hug and thanked them.

She said that they made a perfect team.

The Sheriff came over and thanked them for having done the heavy work.

He then asked for their weapons.

He then let her know that a deputy would drive them back to their car. He made the point that this same deputy would have extra weapons in case they were attacked.

Alex called the Chief. She received a message that he would call back after he, Bill and Trevor got through studying the video that had been sent to him.

Alex had her phone on audio and watched as Trey and Sandra nodded their heads.

Alex asked Trey to drive back to the hotel. She took off her vest and looked at the side and the back of her bullet proof vest and pointed to two hits she had taken.

Trey looked at her, shook his head, and asked if she was OK.

Alex nodded in the affirmative and said that she was now thoroughly bruised on all sides. She said she was looking forward to the next two weeks on desk duty.

The three of them were having lunch when the Chief called back. He congratulated them on a successful visit to Mississippi.

He said the video captured by their target group seemed like an action video put together to show three superheroes working together.

He went on to let them know that he had a special desk job assignment for each of them.

They were to report to the gun range for two weeks of training duty.

They were going to train everyone on how to shoot.

Alex laughed about her new desk job. She looked at Trey and Sandra and gave them a thumbs up.

The End

Preview of: Votive Candles

<u>1 A Step Outside</u>

Alex sipped on her drink and looked at Matt. He quizilled his eyebrows as he took in her gaze and took a sip of his drink. She smiled and explained that she was thinking about the last case and how significantly being a victim of a hate crime had affected her.

She said that it was the first time she had thought of herself as a victim.

She explained that it had caught her unprepared to be attacked for her color. She had come to expect and handle all forms of discrimination but had not anticipated someone trying to kill her for being Black.

She knew that her survival did not change the fact that a significant number of such people continued hold onto their hateful beliefs.

She was sure their own insecurities fueled their beliefs and attitudes.

She added that their enrollment at the university in the class on the History of the Black experience in the building of America was really refreshing her memory and it was broadening her understanding of what their race had endured.

She made the point that even as they endured they had made significant contributions to the growth of the country.

She realized that being one of only four students in an all-white school and being raised in an all-white affluent neighborhood made her experience closer to being white than being black.

Throughout her growing up she had periodically sensed and experienced social discrimination but in what she now realized was a much more subdued fashion than the majority of persons of color.

Her continuing higher education had also lifted her up to a social level where discrimination was practiced in a subtle manner.

The fact that no long term Cincinnati police member had been willing to be her partner in the detective unit was another time that discrimination was blatantly obvious.

Trey had been hired into the detective unit because he said he preferred to be second on the team and that person's color did not matter.

She had immediately known that he would be the person she could count on. He had been a Marine that had fought in Iran and had seen battle. He had been recognized for his bravery and had been awarded the purple heart. From their first meeting she felt that they would make a great team.

She had been repeatedly attacked by gunmen trying to kill her. She had been lucky, and her personal skill had made them all pay the ultimate price.

Every time she need backup, Trey was there

She told Matt that it had been a quiet period at work and that she knew that the Chief was guiding most of the work away from her.

He was in his protective mode.

She had welcomed this but was now ready to get back to the work she loved.

She shared that, Trey, her work partner, had commented that he had spent more time with family in the last few weeks and that she should get attacked more often.

She had replied that she loved him too.

The two of them had become a team that was looked upon as the top team in the detective unit.

Even Trevor, with whom she sparred verbally every time they were around each other had complimented her on the way she handled her cases.

She and Trey were both AA members and supported each other in staying on the dry side. She had been an AA member since her college days and over a year of working with Trey she had gotten him to join. It had made a difference for him, and he thanked her for her persistence in getting him to go with her.

They also spent time with activities that reduced the stress of their jobs.

Alex was "Aunt Alex" to Trey's son Nolan. She and his wife, Lindsey, were good friends. They often had lunch, and it seemed that two weekends a month, Alex and Matt were over to Trey's house for dinner.

Annie, the young woman she had rescued from her fifteen-year captivity in the Pennsylvania forest, now a very successful, wealthy artist and her two daughters, Linda and Lorie were often at these gatherings at Trey's.

Both of the girls also referred to her as, "Aunt Alex."

Annie had recently purchased a home on seven and a half acres in Indian Hill. The housewarming had been a grand event. Annie had thanked Alex for saving her and for getting her into painting professionally.

Alex brought her mind back to Matt and took in his green eyes and smiled. She was surrounded by the people she loved and who gave her inner power and inspiration.

She thought to herself, "What more could a person want?"

She had made a point of supporting one of the best restaurants in Cincinnati because it had been the scene of her first shooting.

This evening, she was sitting at the same table and facing in the same direction as the time she had been attacked.

Her weapon was in her purse.

She had put the purse straps on her chair and had sat on them so that the purse acted as a holster.

She suddenly realized that someone was walking toward her table. She quietly told Matt to do exactly as she told him.

She made certain that the individual was not brandishing a weapon. He was well dressed and had a smile on his face.

She still put her hand on her weapon.

He excused his interruption and introduced himself as John Williams. He explained that he had come to dinner with his companion. He pointed to a very good-looking lady sitting alone at a table and introduced her as Hanna Hillman. He went on to say that he had recognized the two of them because of the news casts in which they had both recently appeared.

He stopped and then declared that he need her help and would she consider doing some investigation to bring two criminals to justice.

Alex released the grip on the revolver in her purse. She had never been approached in quiet this manner. She was intrigued but she made the point that her assignments were given to her by her boss, and that John should contact the Cincinnati Chief of Detectives, Bruce Johnson.

John looked at her and knew that he had to provide enough information so that she would take on his case. He replied that he had already made an official request that would most likely be in the Chief's hand by Monday morning. He asked if he could sit for a moment and explain why he needed her to take the case.

Alex pointed to the chair to her right and said he had five minutes.

She watched as John's face took on a strained look. She immediately sensed that the case had a personal aspect to it.

She listened as he explained that the request was in two parts. One was to find and return a Priest that had failed to respond to a Grand Jury subpoena. The priest was being charged for being a pedophile. John explained that he had been an Altar boy in the church and had been one of the young boys that had been a victim of this priest. He had removed himself from the case and Hanna was now handling it. There were three persons that were potential witnesses.

This was the part of his request that he most wanted help with. It was to find and return this priest to face the Grand Jury and hopefully then be brought in front of a jury of his peers and be tried for his crime.

He said the second help request was due to a lawyer that she should be somewhat familiar with, a Samuel Ellington III.

This was a case that he was personally handling that consisted of a peculiar divorce situation. A wealthy individual and his wife were in the process of getting a divorce. It was a friendly split, and she was to receive half of their combined wealth. During the divorce she died but there were certain indications that there may have been foul play. John explained that he had reviewed the divorce agreement, and everything was fair and equitable. His client had put his deceased wife's portion into a Charity Remainder Trust that would allocate its money and give it to a charity that she had always supported.

The situation was that Samuel Ellington III had accused his client, the husband, of murder and of illegally retaining control of her wealth.

The help he was asking for was for Alex to use her investigative skill to find out who was behind the charge and who would benefit financially if the money that was in the Charity Remainder Trust was released to them.

Alex looked at John and smiled. She quietly informed John that she would consider taking the cases if they came officially to her.

She also let him know that she was just recovering from a hate crime and knew how hard it was to get over feeling like a victim.

John thanked her and asked if he could buy the two of them a drink.

Alex smiled, thanked him for the offer, and let him know that both their drinks were Pellegrino and she pointed to a large bottle that was still half full and declined the offer.

John said that it was a pleasure talking to her, thanked her and returned to his table.

Matt looked at her and asked if she thought the case would make it to the Chief's desk.

Alex looked across the room to where John was sitting down across from his companion. She replied that it would be a first, but she figured that John was the type of person that knew how to work the legal system. He had the same presence as her mother who was also a lawyer that was mostly on the winning side.

That Sunday, Alex for some unknown reason, decided to attend Mass.

It was the first time since she had moved to Cincinnati.

She went in early.

She lit a Votive candle and made a prayer for guidance.

She wanted guidance on whether to pursue the wayward priest.

The nightmare she had experienced about this situation was one where she was the victim.

She decided to light a second Votive candle and ask for guidance on her romance with Matt.

Her relationship was one that she cherished and wanted to keep growing.

She sat through a sermon and realized that hearing the same story over and over was why she had stopped going to Mass. She was sure she had heard every version of sermon and every twist that the priests tried to enlist in giving a fresh sermon.

They needed the help of some good writers.

2 The Choice

Johnnie thought back on how his relationship with Alex had changed his life. He had returned from Vietnam and had been rejected by a society that he had fought for in a country that he had never heard of against a people that as a famous black boxer had said and went to jail for, "the people in Vietnam are not a threat to the United States."

He had worked hard at every job that he had been able to land but seemed to be the first to be laid off when business went south.

He did not realize that when he had witnessed the brutal killing of a young lady that his life had taken an upward turn.

He was sure he would be dead within a couple of weeks.

When the wrong person was arrested for the killing, he knew he had to come forward and correct the error.

He was rejected by an ass of a lawyer with the ridiculous name of Samuel Ellington III that was representing the man accused of murder. He wondered if he was the third ass in his family.

After being ignored, he had then remembered the young black rider that passed the Cincinnati Library on a bicycle early each morning. He knew she was a cop because he had followed her and watched her lock her bike into the bike rack at the entrance to the police station.

He had stopped her and told her his story.

She had believed him.

She had hired him as her part time computer analyst.

She had gotten him his apartment superintendent job in the apartment building that she lived in.

She had changed the downward trajectory of his life.

She had saved him.

The recent attack on her because she was black had enraged him and he had worked harder than he had ever done before to make sure that the attackers were brought to justice.

As he expected Alex closed that case and was now recovering. He knew that she was seeing an psychologist to deal with the fact that she had been a victim just because of her color.

He had decided that he would take a personal hand in trying to keep her safe. He had decided to use some of his Vietnam experience as the point person on a march and became the point bicycle rider on Alex's way to work.

This morning, he was outfitted in a purple and black riding outfit. He was her lead on her ride to work. He had spent a small fortune on his bike.

It was a different brand but of the same caliber that Alex rode.

He had declared that he was protecting his lifestyle and that she would have a riding partner for as long as he could pedal.

He had been surprised when Alex had thanked him and had purchased a bike stand for him as a gift.

Johnnie insisted that they would alternate making the choice of the route they would take to work.

He also insisted that he be the point person. He pointed out that it had been his role in Vietnam, and he had survived it. His only demand was that he got to have the donut of his choice once they got to the station and that he was assigned a desk near her and Trey.

Alex laughed and agreed to his demands. She made the point that she would probably not have survived in Vietnam and from what she knew the women from North Vietnam were fierce fighters that would have challenged her.

She welcomed Johnnies partnership. She was still struggling to overcome the feeling of being a victim of a hate crime. Her sessions with the department psychologist were continuing but she had pushed them to be done either at a lunch session or in morning coffee break session.

Her psychologist was slowly becoming a friend.

The sessions helped her, and it helped with her AA adherence. She had enlisted Trey for periodic participation in her meetings with her psychologist.

He had commented that it helped him as well.

This Monday morning after changing into her work clothes she sat down and was sipping her coffee.

Trey walked in with his cup and a half of a bear claw. He handed the other half to her.

Johnnie had a jelly filled donut well on the way to completion.

Bill and Trevor had their coffee and donuts.

The five of them were sharing their normal morning banter when the volume from the Chief office caused them to stop and look at each other.

Trevor asked if Alex's car was still in the lot and that it had not been blown up.

Bill commented that a new case that the Chief was not in agreement with had probably arrived on his desk.

Alex looked down at her coffee but remained silent. She wanted to call Matt and let him know that John's case had made it to the Chief.

She wondered how it had been delivered. Usually, the cases came from the coroner after a killing. This one was coming into the Chief in a form that seemed to anger him.

After what seemed like a moment of eternity the Chief opened his office door, pointed to Alex, and asked her to come in.

Alex listened to Bill as he said to remember that she had four people that would back up any decision she made. She quietly thanked him as she put her coffee down and turned to go into the Chief's office.

The Chief asked her to sit down so that he could explain a request that had come to his office. He had told his boss that he would leave the choice as to whether to take the case up to her. He said that line had caused his boss to get upset and threaten him.

Alex looked at the Chief and smiled and replied that of course she would take the case.

She had to keep his reputation intact.

He looked at her and asked how she could be sure she would take the case before she had even heard what it was.

She replied that she had gone to church for the first time since coming to Cincinnati and had received guidance that she was to take the case.

The Chief shook his head. He asked if she knew what the request was.

She replied that she would like to hear his take on it.

They both sat silently for a moment.

She was relieved when he opened a file that had a formal looking document that provided a written request. She wanted to understand the request in detail and how success would be measured.

The Chief looked at her and asked if he could call in the rest of her team so that he would only have to go through the details one time.

Alex nodded her head in agreement. She knew she would need the support of every one of the four sitting outside.

The Chief signaled for the rest to come in. He waited until everyone was seated. He commented that the assignment was different from their usual approach.

Trevor commented that it really must be since the office had been silent since Alex had been called in. He went on that usually everyone sitting outside hoped that the windows didn't blow out.

The Chief looked at him and nodded and replied that he had a mop and bucket assignment that would suit Trevor.

Then he opened the folder in front of him and slowly read the request.

Alex had turned her chair so that she could watch the four.

Bill gave small whistle as he listened to the details.

She saw Trevor's face go a little pale when the Chief went into the details that covered a Father Chris. She understood his reaction because she knew that he had been an Altar boy in his church and had asked his son if he would be interested.

The Chief pointed to Alex and shared that he was leaving the decision to her.

Alex nodded and said that it was a case that had come to her and had been explained by the person making the request. It had driven her to go to Church to ask for guidance. She shared that she had lit a Motive Candle and made a prayer.

It had been answered.

She asked if anyone had any questions.

Bill nodded and asked what he and Trevor should do.

Trevor commented that as always he had her back.

Johnnie smiled and replied that he already knew what her miracle request was going to be. He would get right on it once he walked his bicycle back to his apartment.

The Chief look at her and commented that he would cover the politics of the situation. He was a little upset at the route that the request had taken, and he wanted to know more about John Williams.

Alex looked at him and suggested that the politics would probably center on someone that had it in for John.

She suggested that the two of them work closely together to ensure that the top of the food chain was addressed versus the one asking for help.

She was sure that John had not divulged his own experience with Father Chris, and she said nothing about it.

She looked at Johnnie and said that she would need to find Father Chris's location.

She also wanted to know who was involved in the other part of the case that dealt with the money involved in the divorce case.

She added that Father Chris's location was the priority.

She looked at Bill and Travor and asked them to work with Johnnie and handle the money case.

She looked at Trey and said she needed his support on the religious side of the case.

She asked if anyone had an objection to calling the case, the Case of the Votive candles.

Travis commented that he was Baptist and wanted everyone to know he knew what Votive candles were and that he had never believed in them, but he was OK with giving the case that name.

Bill just shook his head and commented, "I put up with this guy every day."

Alex nodded and thanked the Chief for the gesture of letting her choose but like he often said, "things seem to come from above."

Not only did help come from above but Alex was soon to find out that it would also come from "the Angle on the Hill.

Thank You for reading this far.

Purchase Votive Candles at

https://Remwriter95.net/

About the Author

Ronald E. Mueller
remwriter95@gmail.com

Ron grew up in what is now Flint River State Park in Southeast Iowa. The 170-year-old house Ron lived in is built into a hillside. It faces a 125-foot-high cliff towering over the little Flint River. The house and the land talked to him about; the passing of time, the struggle to conquer the land, the struggles people faced and the wonder of nature.

He climbed the cliffs, crawled into the caves, dove from the swimming rock, collected clams from the bottom of the pond, gigged and skinned frogs for their legs. He trapped muskrats for fur, hunted raccoon in the dead of night, and with only a stick hunted rabbits in the dead of winter.

His young life was outdoors, and nature tested him.

He walked to a one room stone schoolhouse uphill both ways. A stern but warm-hearted teacher, Mrs. Henry was instrumental in shaping his character as she shepherded him from the fourth to the eighth grade.

It was a great way to grow up.

Ron graduated from Burlington, High School, went to Vietnam in the Navy. He graduated from The University of South Florida with an master's degree in engineering, worked for thirty eight years for Procter and Gamble, traveled around the world thirty times.

He has remained happily married for more than fifty years. His daughter and his two sons are all successful and his three grandchildren have all graduated.

His wife has humored and supported him as he became a full time professional story teller.

His experiences inter-twined with snippets of fantasy lend themselves to the adventures he leads the reader through.

Books by Ron Mueller

Fiction Series
The Alex Evercrest Series
The River Front
The Girl on The Grill
Missing
Maggot
Racist
Votive Candles
Windy City
Country Road
Pool of Blood
Sins of the Daughter
Body Parts
The Skull Collector
The Vanishing
The Shadow Fighter
Moonshine
Grief's Trajectory
The Magic Touch
Northern Lights
Alex Evercrest Heroine
Alex Evercrest Collection Two
New Direction
A Family Affair
Disruption
The St. Lebuinnus Church Murder

A Brian O'Neil Novel
Hawaiian Phoenix
Moon Curser
Death Broker

The Problem Solver Series
Solutions
Drug Lords
Border Crosser
The Problem Solver Collection

Books by Ron Mueller

<u>The Taelo Series</u>
Taelo: The Early Years
Taelo: The Golden Feather
Taelo: Journey of Discovery
Taelo: Dangerous Passage
Taelo: Condor Clan Slingers
Taelo: Circumvention
Taelo: The Journey of Sages
Taelo: Collection
Taelo: Future Leaders Journey

<u>A Taelo Story:</u>
White Swan and Quiet Pheasant
The Child's Name
Floating Cloud
Quiet Rabbit
Busy Bee
Little Otter & Talking Wren
Broken Spear
Burley Bear & Meadow Flower
Taelo Story Collection

<u>Science Fiction</u>

The Savitar Series:
Journey's End
Savitar
Confluence
Savitar Series Collection

Bram Nielson Series
The Fold
The Message
Fold Wormhole
Negative Fold
Ripples in Time
Bram Nielson Collection

<u>Single Science Fiction Books:</u>
Current Past and Future
The Event
The Door
Viajante 7

Published by: Around the World Publishing LLC.

https://www.Remwriter95.net/